"COME ON, SACK RAT!"

Lorna had almost drifted back to sleep when the pounding started on her door once more. It was obvious that she would get no peace until she gave in to her new mother.

Lorna dragged herself out of bed, pulled on jogging shorts and a tank top, and staggered out of the room. "This had better be the shortest Jazzercise routine in history," she grumbled half-aloud.

She found Mrs. Wheeler prancing around on the pool deck, warming up in a workout suit of electric-green-and-orange graffiti print. To make matters worse, Lorna's stomach had begun growling piteously.

"Just watch me and do what I do," Mrs. Wheeler instructed. "You'll catch on in no time."

Lorna sighed and closed her eyes, thinking longingly of the Markham family tradition of sleeping late on weekends.

Jazzercise at 6:45 in the morning! It was madness. That was all there was to it!

THE
Great Mom
Swap

Betsy Haynes

A Bantam Skylark Book®
Toronto / New York / London / Sydney / Auckland

RL 5, 009-012

THE GREAT MOM SWAP

A Bantam Skylark Book / June 1986

Skylark Books is a registered trademark of Bantam
Books, Inc. Registered in U.S. Patent and
Trademark Office and elsewhere.

ISBN 0-553-15398-6

Published simultaneously in the United States and Canada

Bantam Books are published by Bantam Books, Inc. Its trademark, consisting of the words "Bantam Books" and the por-
trayal of a rooster, is Registered in U.S. Patent and Trademark
Office and in other countries. Marca Registrada. Bantam
Books, Inc., 666 Fifth Avenue, New York, New York 10103.

For Margaret Haynes,
my other mother

1

Lorna Markham threw her shoulders back and stood up straight in front of her dresser mirror, the way her mother was always reminding her to stand.

"Yuk!" she said aloud, making a face at the tall, thin girl with the long, dark hair who looked back at her. Five feet seven inches, she thought with disgust. Not only was she taller than all of the girls in her seventh grade class, she was taller than all of the boys.

She lurched forward into a slump and smiled with satisfaction. Five feet five and a half. An entire quarter inch shorter than Moose Malkovich, star wrestler and all-around jumbo who liked to put a hammerlock on anyone who got in front of him in lunch line.

Turning to one side, Lorna surveyed her slender profile in the mirror. "Not bad," she murmured. Granted, she looked a teensy bit better when she stood up straight, but it certainly wasn't worth all the grief she got from her mother.

"For goodness' sake, Lorna. Stand up straight," her mother would always say. She was an absolute broken record. "You're a tall Texan. Square your shoulders and be proud of yourself."

That was all right for Ann Markham to say. She wasn't the giraffe of Colleyville Junior High. She was only five feet six, which was why she didn't understand how awful it felt to tower over every living creature.

Her mom had been hassling her again at breakfast.

"I really don't understand why you slump like that, Lorna," her mother said. "Look at all the great women in history who were tall."

"Like who?" Lorna grumbled. She was unbelievably tired of the subject.

"Well—" Her mother thought for a moment. Then she brightened and said, "Eleanor Roosevelt! Now there was a woman who was tall and proud of it!"

Lorna nearly choked on her toast. "Eleanor Roosevelt, for Pete's sake! What makes you think I want to be like her?"

"Oh, you don't have to be exactly like her," Mrs. Markham assured her. "In fact, you can be anything you want to be. Like I've said before, you're lucky to have been born in the right generation."

Lorna groaned to herself and prepared for what she knew was coming next.

"In my job with Office Temps I can't help but notice the younger women making their way up the corporate ladder and taking advantage of opportunities that were never available to me. All you have to do is maximize your potential. Just look at your best friend. Scotti maximizes her potential. She wants to be a writer, and she has already had an article published in the local newspaper." Moving closer to Lorna, she said in very serious tones, "Above all, be anything you want to be."

Lorna sighed and didn't answer. What she wanted to be was short.

Now, back in her room, a soft knock sounded at her door. Lorna shot up straight again before she called, "Who is it?"

"It's me. Scotti."

"I'm coming," Lorna answered. Picking up her school books and her lunch, Lorna reached for the knob just as the door burst open and her best friend slid in and backed against the door, shutting it behind her. Scotti was slightly overweight and only four feet eleven and three-quarters inches tall, the perfect size according to Lorna. Scotti never got a stiff neck from looking down at everybody all day long, and the boys all thought she was cute. If I didn't like her so much, Lorna often thought, I would absolutely hate her.

Scotti was breathless from dashing out her own backdoor, through the gate in the stockade fence that separated their backyards, and into the Markham house just as she had done every school morning since she moved to Texas four years ago. The two of them had immediately become best friends. "It's ten whole minutes until bus time," she paused, dramatically widening her already large blue eyes, "and I'm desperate."

Fishing around in her knapsack, Scotti extracted a badly mashed chocolate bar. "You wouldn't believe the gross concoction we had for breakfast," she said as she carefully dug slivers of paper out of the candy with her long purple fingernails. "Mom called it Oriental Sunrise Delight, and it was scrambled eggs full of onions, green pepper, mushrooms, and of course bean sprouts. She never serves anything without BEAN SPROUTS. It was totally gross."

"But I'll bet it was nonfattening and very nutritious," said Lorna with a chuckle. Scotti's mother was an absolute health nut and served the weirdest food in the world, which was why Scotti kept little caches of food hidden in her closet, in her locker at school, and even in the bottom of her knapsack. She called them her survival kits.

Scotti devoured the candy in one gigantic bite. Then she closed her eyes and fell back across Lorna's bed, sighing with contentment. An instant later her eyes popped open and she sat up, frowning. "Do you know what's so weird, Lorna? Mom's always griping about my improper eating habits, as she calls them, and going into her mood-food routine about how chocolate is a depressant and how I'm probably stunting my growth by not eating right. Then she says how skinny I would be if I took her advice. You would think she could figure out that if she served something edible at mealtime, I might not eat so much junk."

"Fat chance," said Lorna with a chuckle. "Come on. It's time for the bus."

Raking her fingers through her short blond curls as she passed the mirror, Scotti followed Lorna out of the house like a miniature shadow.

"If you want my opinion," Scotti said as they stopped at the end of the driveway to wait for the school bus, "I have always thought that every mother in the world has a copy of a book entitled *A Hundred and One Ways to Hassle Your Child*. And it lists all the rules for driving your kid berserk."

Lorna's eyes brightened as she nodded in agreement. "I'll bet you're right. And I'll bet I know where they get them. At the hospital. They're in those plastic bags they give all new mothers along with the free samples of baby powder and disposable diapers."

"And the doctors and nurses make them swear a solemn oath to use those books or they can't take home their new babies," Scotti added dramatically.

"Rule one," said Lorna, pointing her finger for emphasis. "Criticize every single thing your child does, no matter how insignificant."

"Rule two," Scotti said with mock seriousness. "Never agree with your child's opinion on any subject. Always point out that she is wrong."

Lorna thought a minute. "Don't ever give your child a chance to do something when she gets the time. Meet her at the door and yell, 'Why isn't your homework done?' and 'When are you going to clean your room?'"

"Don't forget rule four," said Scotti. "Don't ever let your child just relax and live comfortably in her room. Insist that everything is hung up or put away and that it is totally germ-free."

Lorna was right on cue. "Make a federal case of leaving a towel on the bathroom floor."

"Always embarrass your child by saying dumb things in front of her friends, especially if her friends happen to be cute boys."

"Never let her communicate by telephone with another member of her own generation for longer than it takes to say hello and good-bye."

"Insist that she keep her stereo turned down so low that she gets ear strain trying to hear it."

"Speaking of ear strain, here comes chaos," said Scotti, nodding in the direction of the lumbering yellow school bus that was making its noisy way up the quiet, tree-lined street. The driver, Jim Cooper, didn't care how much noise the kids made as long as they stayed in their seats, so you could usually hear the bus coming at least a block away.

"It's time," Lorna said solemnly. "Are you ready?"

Scotti nodded. "My dog's shinier than your dog," she sang, just as she did every morning when the school bus rounded the corner onto Allendale.

"My dad can beat up your dad," Lorna sang back.

Then, as they climbed onto the bus together and at the top of their lungs they sang, "MY MOM'S CRABBIER THAN YOUR MOM!"

2

Dianna struggled to open her eyes, but it felt as if her long, spidery lashes were intertwined like fingers of steel, locking her lids together. Lying pale and beautiful among the satin pillows on the great canopy bed, Dianna could hear soft voices murmuring nearby.

"She can't die! Not beautiful Dianna!"

"It will be all Maude's fault. How can that woman treat her daughter so wickedly?"

"Just look at poor Dianna. She's so lovely."

"And so kind."

"And so sincere."

"Scotti! Are you in your room? You'd better not

be working on that novel again unless your home-work is done."

Scotti looked up with a start. She had been so engrossed in her writing that she had completely for-gotten the time. It was nearly five o'clock, the time her mother always returned from her six-mile run. Except, that is, for those days when she was flying. Scotti's mother, Helene, was a flight attendant and her father, Captain Craig Wheeler, was a pilot.

"Sure, Maude," she muttered under her breath, but aloud she called, "It's okay, Mom. I'm doing my homework now."

With a sigh Scotti closed the ring binder that held her precious novel *Prisoner of Fate* and stashed it in the back of her closet beside the shoebox containing three Reese's Peanut Butter Cups, four Snickers bars, and a bag of M&M's. *Prisoner of Fate* was an epic novel set in the romantic 1700's and was about the lovely Dianna—who bore a striking resemblance to Scotti herself—and the tragic circumstances that befell her at the hands of her mother, Maude the Tyrant. It was all fiction, of course, and she had begun writing it the year before, after she had read *Flowers in the Attic*, by V. C. Andrews. In that book a brother and sister were hidden away for years in the attic of their grandmother's house by their wicked, selfish mother. Scotti had cried and cried over their story. Of course, she had never been imprisoned in an attic, and she didn't have a brother. But, just the same, she knew how they must have felt. After all, her own mother could be such a pain at times. Like right now.

Reluctantly, she went back to her desk and her homework, stopping just long enough to scoop a Snickers bar out of the shoebox. She needed fortification if she was going to face that social studies book. Besides, she thought, Mom will probably have something fantastic for dinner, like broiled squid and a spinach soufflé, or zucchini lasagna with clam sauce. Health food—YUK!

Scotti raced through the questions at the end of the social studies chapter that Mr. Deweese had assigned. She was thankful that there was only one more week of school left before summer vacation, when she planned to get plenty of serious writing done on *Prisoner of Fate*. Her mother would be hassling her as usual not to spend so much time in her room. "Stop lying around so much," her mother loved to say. "Get out into the fresh air and sunshine. Exercise! Eat healthful foods. It's good for both your mind and your body."

She smiled slyly at the thought. There were three perfectly good reasons why she spent so much time in her room: One: To avoid exercise. Two: To nibble away at the secret supply of food in her closet without being detected and forced to consume tofu and bean sprouts. And Three: To work on *Prisoner of Fate*.

The sound of laughter broke into her thoughts. Someone was in the kitchen with her mother, and they were laughing up a storm. Scotti slammed her social studies book shut and frowned at her closed door. It could only be one person: Lorna Markham.

"What she finds to laugh about all the time with

my mother is a mystery to me," Scotti muttered. "But I suppose there is something a little bit weird about everybody."

She left her room and marched up the hall, across the carpeted den, and into the kitchen to find her mother and her best friend holding onto the counter, convulsed with laughter. Lorna was so doubled over that she was barely taller than Scotti's five-feet, two-inch mother.

"What's going on in here?" Scotti demanded in mock seriousness. "Why are you two so rowdy?" Still, she couldn't help but smile at how funny they looked.

Mrs. Wheeler pointed to the large wooden cutting board covered with vegetables that lay between herself and Lorna on the counter. She started to speak but was stopped by another spasm of laughter. Lorna looked on helplessly, a hand across her mouth as if to trap the mirth inside. Finally, Mrs. Wheeler wiped her eyes and said haltingly, "She came over . . . looking for you . . . but when she . . . saw . . . I was chopping . . . veggies . . . she asked if I wanted her to MUSH THE MINCEROOMS!" With that Scotti's mother let out another shriek of laughter.

"And cel the dicery," Lorna shouted between giggling fits. "And carr the slicots."

"Okay, okay, you two. Settle down," said Scotti, trying to mock her mother when she was in a serious mood. But the laughter filling the air had a contagious effect, and soon Scotti was giggling along with them.

"It was just one of those crazy things that sounded so funny when it happened," offered Mrs.

Wheeler. Then she gestured toward the girls as another giggle burst from her lips. "Run along, you two, or I'll never get dinner on the table."

Retreating to Scotti's bedroom, they closed the door and Lorna collapsed into the rocker by the window like a puppet whose strings had suddenly been cut. Scotti sank to the carpeted floor beside her.

"Scotti, your mother is an absolute riot. She has a fabulous sense of humor."

"Oh, brother," said Scotti, rolling her eyes toward the ceiling. "She wouldn't have thought it was the least bit funny if I had said it. Mushing the mincerooms! She wouldn't have even cracked a smile."

"That's because you wouldn't have said it," Lorna quipped. "You know how you hate to help your mother in the kitchen. Of course, I'm not so crazy about helping mine either, but your mother's different. She's a riot."

"You already said that," said Scotti in a pouty voice. "But your mother at least listens to what a person has to say while they're helping her. She listens to me whenever I set the table for her. Mine keeps a running lecture going on the evils of sweets and sedentary living. That's her new favorite word, 'sedentary.' Besides, your mother has such a cute accent. I love to hear her talk."

"That's a TEXAS accent, you airhead. That's where you live. Remember? Texas? It's just that since all you Yankees moved down here, you hardly ever hear the English language spoken properly."

"And that's why we allow your family to live in

our Yankee ghetto," Scotti teased. "You're our token Texans. You add charm to our neighborhood full of Northerners. Seriously, though," she added in a quiet voice. "Have you ever noticed how much better we get along with each other's mother?"

Lorna was thoughtful for a moment. "No, not until you mentioned it," she said. "But it is true, isn't it? My mom never hassles you, but whenever I'm around it's always 'Stand up straight.' 'Maximize your potential.' 'Be anything you want to be.' Blah, blah, blah."

Scotti giggled. "All I ever hear from my mother is 'Exercise and eat healthy food.' 'Fit, not fat.' She always says, 'Look at your best friend. Lorna's so thin. She must have found the perfect balance between exercise and nutrition.'"

"Oh, I hear about you, too," Lorna added quickly. "'Scotti maximizes her potential. She wants to be a writer, and she's already had an article published.' I must have heard about that one measly article about our neighbor Mr. Killington and the airplane he built in his backyard at least a million times. I've even thought of telling her about *Prisoner of Fate* just to give her something different to talk about."

"You do and I'll kill you," shouted Scotti, whizzing a stuffed unicorn past Lorna's left ear. "Even my mother doesn't know the name of it or what it's about. All she knows is that I'm writing a novel, and that's more than enough. What I really should do is work on it at your house. Your mother is interested in my writing, and she wouldn't fuss at me about it all the time."

"Hey, that's a great idea," said Lorna. "And I could come over here and slump to my heart's content. Your mother is a lot of fun to be around, and she has never once told me to stand up straight."

"Of course not. She thinks you're perfect," said Scotti. Then her eyes widened as a delicious thought struck. "I have an even better idea! And you know, Lorna, it just might work."

"What might work?"

"Swapping moms!"

"Swapping moms?" Lorna echoed.

"Sure. School will be out in a week. I could move into your house and you could move into mine. We could live in each other's rooms. We practically do anyway. And just think. With your mom and dad and your older brother and little sister influencing me all the time, I'd turn into a real Texan and probably start saying 'y'all.' And you would become the only child of the king and queen of jet lag. But most important"— Scotti paused and pointed a finger at her friend for emphasis—"neither of our mothers would have anyone to hassle, and you and I would have PEACE! We could call it the Great Mom Swap."

Lorna's mouth dropped open and then spread into a wide grin. "Scotti, you're a genius! An absolute genius!"

"You're not the only one who's perfect," Scotti teased. "Now all we have to do is come up with a plan to convince our parents to let us do it."

3

The girls designated Wednesday after school as "Plan Time." They would meet in Scotti's backyard, sunbathe beside the Wheelers' swimming pool, and exchange all of the fabulous ideas they had come up with for convincing their parents to let them trade places. It sounded like a cinch.

The first thing to go wrong was that Scotti's mother was in the pool when they arrived.

"There goes our privacy," grumbled Lorna as she spread her beach towel on the pool deck and dropped onto her stomach. "I thought she always ran at this time of day."

"She does," conceded Scotti. "Usually." Scotti stood at the pool's edge watching her mother glide gracefully back and forth through the water. "She's doing laps. She must have decided that it was too hot to run this afternoon."

"Sounds like a Yankee," Lorna teased, shaking her head sadly. "Just couldn't take it, I guess."

Scotti kicked imaginary sand at her friend and stretched out on her own beach towel. "Don't worry. She can't hear us when she's swimming. We'll just be careful to change the subject when she comes out of the water."

"Listen. I have a great idea," Lorna said brightly. "We'll tell our parents that we're doing a project for the family living unit of our health class. We really are on the family living unit, and we can tell them that we have to observe another family and write a report."

Scotti wrinkled her nose. "After school's out?"

"We can say we're supposed to do it over summer vacation," Lorna offered.

"That would never work. When would we get graded on this alleged report? Not after school's out, and we won't be taking health next year."

Lorna sighed. "You're right. So much for my fabulous idea. What did you come up with?"

"Well," Scotti began. "Since my parents are both with the airlines and they're really big on travel, I thought maybe I could convince them that my greatest ambition is to become a foreign exchange student when I get to high school. I could tell them that you want to be one too, and that we have decided it would be a valuable experience if we practiced living with each other's family."

Lorna had a puzzled look on her face. "Would you run that by me again?" she asked. Then, shaking her head, she said, "No. I think I've got it. Correct me if I'm wrong. We're going to convince our parents that moving into each other's rooms would be like becoming foreign exchange students? You've got to be kidding."

"It's no worse than your idea," Scotti pouted.

"Looks like it's back to the drawing board," said Lorna.

Just then Mrs. Wheeler stepped out of the pool. For the millionth time Lorna was struck by her youthful appearance and gorgeous figure. She looked more like Scotti's sister than her mother. I'll bet men passengers make passes at her all the time, thought Lorna. Grabbing the towel off the back of a nearby lounge chair, Mrs. Wheeler patted her face and smiled at the girls.

"You two should go for a swim. The water is wonderful. Really invigorating."

"Brrrr," said Lorna.

"I'm not into invigorating," said Scotti. "Actually, I'm into languid. Let me know when it's like bathwater."

"You wouldn't have to worry about those extra pounds if you got more exercise, Scotti," chirped her mother.

"Who's worried?" muttered Scotti so softly that only Lorna could hear.

"You know, people as short as we are have to be especially careful because every single ounce shows. Now people like Lorna"—she paused, flashing a brilliant smile in Lorna's direction—"have more space to distribute extra weight. But besides the exercise, swimming is fun!" With that Mrs. Wheeler flipped her towel over her shoulder and headed for the house, leaving Scotti scowling at her back.

"Now people like Lorna," Scotti mimicked her mother, "are totally perfect." Then with a sigh she added, "Come on, Lorna. Let's get to work on our plans. The situation is getting critical."

For the next two days neither girl came up with a single idea. Suddenly, it was Friday, the last day of school before summer. The girls were cleaning out the locker they shared, tossing things to be discarded into a pile on the floor and stuffing everything else into their knapsacks. To Scotti's great delight, she found an unopened package of chocolate chip cookies underneath her gym shorts. Tearing the package open, she said with a sigh, "Come on, Lorna. Help me eat these. If I take them home and Mom finds them, I'm sunk."

"Don't worry," said Lorna. "You can hide any you have left at my house. My mom won't care. Besides, you'll be living in my room soon anyway IF we can come up with a plan."

"I keep telling you, the foreign exchange idea will work. I know it will, if we handle it right. Obviously, we won't be speaking another language or anything like that. We'll simply be adapting to another family's life-style."

"But Scotti. We're neighbors. Our parents cook out together on weekends. Our life-styles aren't that different."

"That's what you think," Scotti said with a

snicker. "You've never lived with an airline family."

Lorna thought that over for a moment. It was true that Scotti's parents had really strange schedules. They would fly off in the middle of the night sometimes and stay away for days, only to come back and be around the house even longer. It always seemed weird to go to Scotti's house in the middle of the afternoon when other fathers were at work and find Captain Wheeler puttering around in his yard. But how hard could that be to get used to? she wondered.

"I guess you're right," she conceded, grinning slyly. "I mean for you it will be like another language with everybody saying 'y'all' and speaking in that cute Texas accent all the time. But don't worry. I'll be available if you need an interpreter."

"Are you game, then?" Scotti demanded. "I know saying we're practicing to be foreign exchange students isn't the greatest idea, but it's the best we've got."

Lorna hesitated, but only for an instant. "I'm game," she said. "Let's each ask them tonight at dinner. How many days or weeks or years should we ask to swap for?"

Scotti's eyes widened. "How about forever?"

"Sounds great to me, but we'd better make it something they'll agree to. How about a couple of weeks?"

"That's probably the max my mom would go for," said Scotti. "If she had to wait more than two weeks to criticize me, I'm sure she would go into withdrawal."

Lorna laughed. "Mine, too. Besides, we can

always ask for an extension if things are going okay.
Shall we ask to change houses tomorrow?"

"Why not? It's Saturday. What else is there to
do?"

The girls shot quick glances at each other as the
same thought struck simultaneously.

"Clean our rooms," Lorna said, making a face.

"You're right," said Scotti. "Yuk! Let's swap
moms instead. Okay?"

Lorna's expression changed to a smile. "It's a
deal!"

4

Squadrons of butterflies were on maneuvers in Lorna's stomach as she squared her shoulders, pulled herself up to her full height, and marched into the kitchen. Her mission was to set the table and, at the same time, to soften up her mother for the BIG QUESTION, which she planned to ask at dinner. She had been racking her brain all afternoon for the right way to lead into it, but so far nothing sounded right. She couldn't remember when she had been so nervous. But that, she assured herself, was because there was so much at stake. If she blew it and her parents said no, she would go on forever being told to stand up straight.

All was peaceful on the field of battle. Her mother had just taken the chicken-fried steak out of the skillet and was slowly stirring the cream gravy with a wooden spoon. So far, so good, Lorna thought.

Chicken-fried steak was her father's favorite meal, and he was due home from work any minute.

Next she glanced into the den where the television blared out the evening news. Her brother, Skip, was lounging on the sofa. One leg was draped over the back and his cowboy hat pulled down over his eyes so that he looked asleep in case his mother thought of any chores he might do. At sixteen, Skip wasn't into chores. He was into cool, and in his opinion it definitely wasn't cool to do chores. Cool was driving around in his copper-colored Camaro with the windows rolled down and the radio turned up. Boys, Lorna thought with disgust.

Suddenly, from out of nowhere, Lorna's six-year-old sister Tiffany streaked by, headed for the den. She was a miniature version of Lorna, with long legs and shoulder-length brown hair. "It's time for the commercial!" she shrieked.

Lorna shook her head and moved aside so that Tiffany could get by. Except for *Sesame Street*, Tiffany's television watching consisted almost exclusively of commercials, and she had an uncanny way of knowing when it was time for one to come on no matter where she was in the house. But even more irritating to Lorna was the way that she knew every single word to every commercial, whether it was toilet bowl cleaners or Toyotas, and she insisted on singing them at the top of her lungs along with the television set.

"BE all that you can BE," Tiffany sang, slightly off key, "in the AR-ar-ar-MEEEE!"

That's it! Lorna thought, jolting so hard that she almost dropped the stack of plates she was carrying to the table. Tiffany and those crazy commercials had just given her the answer.

"Mom," Lorna said a little while later when the entire family was sitting around the table eating dinner. "You know how you're always telling me that I should be whatever I want to be?"

Mrs. Markham's face brightened. "Why yes, darlin'," she said sweetly.

Skip looked at Lorna and raised an eyebrow. Lorna swallowed hard. He could always see through her and know when she was pulling something, but her mother looked convinced, so she went on. "Well, I've been thinking how wonderful it would be to become a foreign exchange student when I get to high school."

Skip suddenly choked on a swallow of milk and clamped a hand over his mouth to keep from spraying the milk all over the table. Lorna knew he was dying to laugh, and she shot him a dirty look and then smiled at her mother.

"Why, Lorna," she cooed. "I had no idea that you had such ambitions. I think that's wonderful. Don't you, Coy?"

Mr. Markham frowned. "What's wrong with Texas?" he demanded. Lorna's father was a tall, lean man who had been born and raised in Texas, and he seldom missed an opportunity to sing the praises of the Lone Star State.

"Nothing, Daddy. I love Texas as much as you

do, but I believe that if I'm going to be all that I can be, I ought to see the world. Being a foreign exchange student would be a wonderful way to see the world and learn about how other people live."

"Why don't you join the Army?" asked Tiffany. "You could be all that you can be in the Army." She was grinning broadly, obviously very proud of her knowledge. "Do you want me to sing the commercial for you?"

"Tiffany, this is different!" Lorna spat out the words and shot her sister a look that definitely meant be quiet but not before Skip jumped into the conversation.

"I think joining the Army is a great idea, Lorna. Basic training is a blast, and you'd love the clothes. You'd get to wear those darling little boots, and the fatigues are out of sight. Besides, if they ever need a flagpole—"

"Mom! Dad! Make him shut up. I'm being serious."

"Your brother is only teasing. Aren't you, Skippy?" Mrs. Markham said. "Besides, it will be another whole year before you'll be in high school, and foreign exchange students are usually juniors or seniors. We have plenty of time to talk about this."

"But Mom, Daddy, that's just the point." Here it comes, she thought. I've got to make this good. "You see, Scotti and I BOTH want to be foreign exchange students. And, Mom, you know how Scotti always maximizes her potential. Well, we've decided that we could maximize our potentials and get valuable experience in learning to adjust to another family's life-style by trading places and living with each other's family for a couple of weeks. It would be great training for when we really do become foreign exchange students."

"Do you mean that Scotti Wheeler would move in here? For two whole weeks?" Skip asked incredulously. Then, holding his hands up in protest, he said, "Oh, no you don't. Not Scotti. Do you realize how spacey she is?"

"She is not spacey," Lorna protested. "She's going to be a famous novelist some day. Besides, she won't bother you."

Lorna felt a tug on her sleeve. "What's spacey?" Tiffany asked in a hoarse whisper. "Is that like an astronaut?"

"Not now, Tiff," Lorna answered. "I'll explain it to you later."

"Then I must be spacey," Tiffany announced proudly. "Because I'm going to be an astronaut, and I'm going to join the Army. BE all that you can BE."

"Hush now, Tiffany. We're having an important discussion," said Mrs. Markham. "Lorna, don't forget that now that school is out, you're responsible for Tiffany on days I work for Office Temps. How are you planning to work that out? Are you planning to take her with you to the Wheelers, or is Scotti going to look after her?"

"That's a good point," her father chimed in. "Scotti is an only child. She might not know how to take care of my little girl."

"Oh, for Pete's sake. She baby-sits all the time, and I'll just be over at her house with nothing but a stockade fence separating our backyards. Besides," Lorna added slyly, "think of what a valuable experience it could be if she stays in a foreign home with small children. She could really say that she has maximized her potential."

"Well—" her mother drawled slowly. She was gazing off into space with a dreamy look on her face. "Of course, we do enjoy having Scotti around. She's so bright and ambitious and hard working and all. And she is such a good writer . . . and, if it's only for two weeks . . ."

"Mom!" Skip agonized.

Mrs. Markham ignored her son. "Why, just think. She might even write an article about our family like the one she wrote about Mr. Killington and the airplane he built in his backyard. You remember that, don't you, Coy?" she asked, turning to her husband.

"Why, yes," said Mr. Markham. "I certainly do. It was a fine article, as I recall."

Lorna's hopes began to swell as her father raised his head a little higher and smiled proudly. It was obvious that he was imagining reading about himself in the newspaper. She couldn't miss an opportunity like this.

"That's right, Mom, Daddy. I'll bet she'd love to write an article about some REAL Texans since she's a Yankee. You could give her lots of good material."

The look on both her parents' faces told Lorna she had won. Later, when she closed her bedroom door behind her and sprawled across her bed, she breathed a huge sigh of relief. She had done it. In spite of Skip, the Army, and Tiffany's talk of being spacey, she had convinced her parents to let her trade places with Scotti for two whole weeks. Reaching for the phone on her bedside table, she dialed the Wheelers' number. Scotti answered after only one ring.

"Scotti! It worked! My parents said okay. What about yours?"

"Mine, too. But boy, I had some anxious moments," confessed Scotti. "I finally got through to my mom when I reminded her that I would really be getting out of my room and eating all kinds of dishes that I'd never tasted before. But the best part was when she said that since everyone in your family is so thin, your parents would be a marvelous influence on me. Those were her very words. Marvelous influence! Isn't that a riot?"

"Yeah, but wait until you hear this. My parents are convinced that you're going to make them famous by writing an article about them like the one you wrote on Mr. Killington for the paper."

At that, they broke into fits of laughter, giggling until they panted from exhaustion.

"Tomorrow?" Lorna finally managed to ask.

"Tomorrow," answered Scotti. "See you then."

They hung up, each dreaming about tomorrow, the big day.

5

_____

Scotti tossed the last of her stuffed animals into a large black plastic leaf bag and surveyed her room one final time. Most of her clothes, her makeup, and her blow dryer were already stacked beside the back-door in preparation for the switch, which would take place in exactly fifteen minutes. The only things left were her shoebox of goodies and her novel, which could both fit easily into the leaf bag. The room looked strangely empty. Scotti felt an unexpected tightness in her throat. Reaching for the ring binder that contained _Prisoner of Fate_, she opened it to a clean page and began to write.

> _Dianna opened her cask of jewels, took out the diamond-and-emerald neck-lace that had been her grandmother's, and wrapped it in silk. Then she placed it in the velvet valise that was open beside her, feel-_

ing an unexpected tightness in her throat.

*It's so strange, she thought. How can I
be sad when freedom is finally mine? I'm no
longer a prisoner of my fate. I'm on my way
to Markham Castle and the new life I've
yearned for.*

*The sound of sobbing arose from
across the room where Maude lay on the
fainting couch, tears streaming down her
face. "Oh, Dianna. My precious daughter.
Surely you aren't going to leave me here,
old, sick, and alone. What ever will I do
when you're gone? Life won't be worth living."*

"Hurry up, Scotti." Her mother's voice startled
her so that she dropped her pencil. "You'd better get a
move on. My new daughter is coming through the
back gate."

Scotti sighed and stuffed the notebook into the
bag with her animals. "So much for Maude sobbing
on the fainting couch," she mumbled. "I think Mom's
actually glad that I'm moving out."

Slinging the bag of animals over her shoulder,
Scotti hurried to the kitchen where Lorna was easing
an armload of clothes through the open door. Then
she bent down and gave Mrs. Wheeler a peck on the
cheek and said, "Hi, Mom. What's for dinner?"

"Spoken like a true daughter," Mrs. Wheeler said
with a laugh. Turning to Scotti she added, "Do you

have everything that you're taking out of your room? Your replacement is here and ready to move in."

Scotti nodded, wincing at the word "replacement."

"Actually, Scotti, the more I think about it, the better the whole project sounds. It will be fun having Lorna with us for a while, and I'm sure you'll enjoy the Markhams." Mrs. Wheeler gave her daughter a knowing smile and added, "One of them in particular."

Scotti flashed a look of anger at her mother. In a moment of pure ecstasy she had confessed to her mother that she had a monster crush on Lorna's brother. The ecstasy had come about when Skip had actually spoken to her and said, "How's it going, kid?" exactly nineteen days ago. He had been strolling down the driveway toward his Camaro, his cowboy hat tilted back on his head, exposing the dark, wavy hair that framed his handsome face. She had been crossing the Markhams' backyard on her way to see Lorna, and was wearing the oldest and most cruddy pair of jeans she owned, naturally. It was the first time he had spoken directly to her and, unable to confide her love to her best friend, Scotti had returned home and poured out every detail to her mother, swearing her to secrecy. Now she was afraid her mother had blown it. But, thank goodness, Lorna had not appeared to notice the insinuation. She headed toward Scotti's room with her armload of clothes, with Mrs. Wheeler still chattering away about the new arrangements.

"And it will be wonderful having someone as nutrition-conscious as Lorna in the house," she was saying. "I have several great new recipes I want to try out now that there will be someone here who will really appreciate them."

"Come on, Scotti. I'll help you get your stuff over to my house," Lorna offered as she came back into the kitchen. "What do you have in this suitcase, anyway? Rocks?"

Ann Markham was waiting by her backdoor when the girls arrived loaded down with Scotti's possessions. She threw her arms around Scotti, stuffed animals, luggage, and all, and gave her a big hug.

"Welcome to our house, darlin'," she said. "We're just going to do everything we can to make you feel at home. Aren't we, Tiffy?"

Tiffany screwed up her face until her lips practically touched her nose and then said in a hurt tone, "I want Lorna. Why does she have to move away?"

"It's just for a little while," Scotti reassured her. "Besides, she'll still be close by, and I'll be here. You and I are good friends, aren't we?"

Tiffany, making sobbing sounds that Scotti knew were definitely fake, ducked behind her mother, and the girls trudged down the hall and deposited their loads on Lorna's bed.

"Whew. I think we got everything of yours in one trip," Lorna said. "And I think that together we can get the rest of my stuff over to your house."

"My records. I forgot my records," said Scotti.

"Eeeks! So did I. Oh, well. We can get them

later. Besides, we have practically the same ones anyway."

As they were loading the last of Lorna's things that were stacked beside the backdoor, Ann Markham reappeared wearing a serious expression. "Now, Lorna. For goodness' sake, don't forget to stand up straight. You never see Helene Wheeler slumping. No, sir. She's too proud of herself, and I want you to be proud of yourself, too. Remember, you're a—"

"Sure, Mom," mumbled Lorna, suppressing a flash of anger. She was determined not to let anything spoil this super moment. "I know. I'm a tall Texan. Come on, Scotti."

Just as the girls left the Markham house, Tiffany popped through the backdoor, waving excitedly. "Say bye-bye to wetness!" she called brightly. "Bye-bye!"

"I didn't know your nickname was Wetness," Scotti teased.

"It isn't. Those are the words to some disposable-diaper commercial. You know, it's the one where the mother says, 'Say bye-bye to wetness,' and the little baby in diapers waves really big and says, 'Bye-bye.' Well, it's Tiff's favorite at the moment."

"Great. So now that I'm living at your house, I suppose I get to be Wetness."

"Probably," Lorna said matter-of-factly. "But don't worry. You'll get used to it."

A little while later, Scotti stood alone in the center of Lorna's room. It was time to unpack her things, but somehow she felt out of place. The room was so different from her own. The wallpaper was awash with bluebonnets, the tiny wildflower that covers Texas hillsides every April, and a large map of the Lone Star State hung on one wall. In fact everything that adorned the room had something to do with Texas. It had never bothered her when she frequently spent the night with Lorna. It had been sort of fun, bobbing around on Lorna's water bed and watching her collection of horse statues cast lifelike shadows on the ceiling. But already Scotti missed the soft pastel walls of her own room and the curving brass headboard of her bed.

She was still standing there when the door burst open and Tiffany entered the room. "I came to help you unpack," she announced and immediately dove for the plastic leaf bag full of animals.

"Hey, wait a minute," yelled Scotti, but she was too late. Tiffany's head and most of her upper body had disappeared into the bag, and stuffed animals were pitching out of it and flying around the room.

"Garfield!" Tiffany shrieked, and she bolted out of the bag waving the familiar yellow cat wearing a bonnet of white satin rabbit ears. It had been Scotti's Easter present from her parents. "Can I keep him? Can I keep him? Oh, Scotti, please!"

"Of course not. He's mine and he's special," Scotti answered angrily. "Now give him to me and pick up the other animals you threw on the floor."

"Then can I help?" Tiffany pleaded. "What's in here?" Before Scotti could answer, Tiffany had opened Scotti's makeup bag and was holding up a bottle of fingernail polish in each hand. "Oh, boy. We can polish my nails."

"TIFFANY!" Scotti shouted. "Get out of my things and get out of this room. Right now!"

With that Tiffany let out a howl and headed for the door. "Mamma!" she cried, slamming it behind her.

Scotti sank to the floor and dropped her chin into her hands. "What have I gotten myself into?" she wondered aloud. There had been times in her life when Scotti had envied Lorna, thinking it would be fun to have a little sister instead of being an only child. On the other hand, Tiffany had always been a pest, and somehow Scotti had thought of her as Lorna's problem. After all, Scotti could always go home to the peace and quiet of her own house when Tiffany became too much of a pain, like now.

Gradually, she began unpacking—hanging her clothes in Lorna's closet, arranging her stuffed animals on Lorna's bed, and setting out her makeup and colognes on Lorna's dresser.

Scotti looked at her watch and was amazed at how late it had gotten. She had spent most of the afternoon getting settled, and now it was almost time for dinner. Brushing her hair carefully, she spread on some light lip gloss and dabbed a little bit of blusher on her cheeks. She wanted to look her best since this would be her first meal with the Markhams—Mr. Markham, Mrs. Markham, Tiffany, and SKIP!

Maybe I should wear a different top, she thought, rummaging through the closet for something special. For the next fifteen minutes she tried on at least a dozen outfits, finally settling on pink cropped pants and a matching pink-and-orange knit top. "Perfect," she whispered to her image in the mirror after she brushed her hair again and added a dot more blusher to each cheek.

Her heart was pounding wildly at the thought of being in the same room with Skip as she opened the door and stepped into the hallway. Self-control! she told herself sternly. After all, as Mom always says, he's only a boy—but what a boy!

Scotti stopped in her tracks, and she felt a fiery heat rise from her neck and spread over her face. Right there in front of her was Skip stepping out of the bathroom directly across the hall. His wet hair was spilling water droplets onto his face, and he was wearing nothing but a large brown bath towel.

"How's it going, kid?"

Skip sauntered down the hall and disappeared into his room, leaving Scotti staring after him as she crumpled against the wall.

6

As soon as Lorna had settled into Scotti's room, she went looking for Mrs. Wheeler. She wasn't in the kitchen, which was no surprise. Not only did Scotti's mother cook light, nutritious meals, she prepared quick ones. No time-consuming roasts or stews. Stir-fried dishes were her specialty, along with lightly broiled fish and steamed vegetables. This was partly because her job as a flight attendant gave her a crazy schedule but mostly because, as Lorna had heard her say more than once, she kept her eating in perspective.

"I'm out here," Mrs. Wheeler called from the patio. She was dressed in raspberry-colored workout clothes with a sweatband around her forehead. She sat atop an exercise bike, pedaling furiously.

Lorna hurried outside to join her. "Thought you might need some help mushing the mincerooms," she said brightly.

"You have a wonderful sense of humor, Lorna," Mrs. Wheeler said. "I know we're going to have a great time having you here." Dropping lightly off the exercise bike, she linked arms with Lorna and headed toward the kitchen. "As a matter of fact, there is something you can help with. I was just getting ready to start dinner."

"Great," said Lorna. "What are we having?"

Mrs. Wheeler beamed at Lorna. "Lasagna, just for you."

"Lasagna?" Lorna asked in surprise. She had not expected anything so totally yummy as lasagna at the Wheeler house.

"That's right. Vegetable lasagna." She bunched her fingertips together and kissed them Italian-style, and said, "Mucho delicious. You're going to love it. You can also help make it. I need you to slice the squash."

"Squash? In lasagna?"

"Vegetable lasagna," Mrs. Wheeler reminded her. "I don't use those terrible noodles that are full of carbohydrates and sugar. I use long slices of summer squash instead. It's light, delicious, and so good for you."

Lorna's spirits plummeted. She knew that Mrs. Wheeler fixed kooky things. After all, she did eat over once in a while. But somehow she had imagined that Scotti's mother would fix normal food while she was staying there. No such luck. Mrs. Wheeler pushed two freshly scrubbed yellow squash across the counter toward her. Vegetable lasagna was what it would be.

Dutifully, Lorna sliced the vegetables while Mrs. Wheeler busied herself concocting the sauce. Lorna tried not to appear bored, but she couldn't get over how quiet it was in the Wheeler house. It was so quiet that she could actually hear the mantel clock ticking in the den. She had always imagined how neat it would be to be an only child like Scotti, but now she wasn't sure. She was used to Tiffany whining at her or Skip picking a fight. It felt natural, and she had to admit that it made helping with meals a lot more fun.

"Do you mind if I go home for a minute?" she asked with a sudden stab of homesickness. "I forgot my clock radio."

"Of course not, dear. Take all the time you need. Dinner won't be ready for a while."

Lorna tried to keep from running across the Wheelers' yard through the gate in the stockade fence and toward her own backdoor. After all, she would feel ridiculous if anyone suspected that she was homesick after only a few hours at her best friend's house.

Bumping through the door with a big grin on her face, Lorna almost tripped over her feet at the sight of Scotti lounging on the sofa in the den like some kind of queen while her mother slaved away in the kitchen. It's no wonder Scotti has a weight problem, thought Lorna, as resentment began to rise. But I'll die before I let her think I'm jealous.

Plastering a fake smile on her face, she called out, "Hi, everybody. I forgot something. Just ignore me. I'll be gone in a second." Waving halfheartedly to

Scotti, she stomped down the hall, jerked the cord to the clock radio out of the plug in the wall, and stuffed the radio under her arm. She wanted to get out of there, even if it meant going back to the tomblike silence of the Wheeler house.

Walking back through the den on her way to the kitchen and the backdoor, Lorna was hit head on by her little sister. Tiffany's skinny little arms circled her hips like steel bands, and she buried her face in Lorna's stomach.

"Oh, Lorna. Please come home. I miss you! I miss you!"

"Sure you do," Lorna said as she pried Tiffany's arms from around her. She started to make some sarcastic remark about Tiff not missing her half as much as she missed Tiff, but at just that moment she inhaled a fantastic aroma. Barbequed brisket. Her favorite. "Wow, Mom. What smells so good?" Then, before she could stop the words, she added, "You're not having brisket, are you? You know that's my favorite."

"Of course we are, darlin'," her mother said, giving Lorna a sympathetic look. "We're having a special supper in honor of Scotti."

"You could stay if you wanted to," Scotti said, but Lorna could tell by the tone of her voice that she didn't really mean it.

"That's okay," Lorna answered stiffly. "Mrs. Wheeler is having a special supper for me, too. I'd better get back. It might be ready."

Then her mother dropped the bomb. "Isn't that nice of her. What is she fixing?"

Lorna thought she would die. She had no choice but to admit the truth. "Vegetable lasagna," she murmured. "It's very nutritious. Well, I'd better go now. Bye."

As she slipped out the backdoor, Lorna was certain that she saw out of the corner of her eye that Scotti was watching her. She's eaten vegetable lasagna. She knows what I have to go through.

It was almost dark when Lorna reentered the Wheelers' house, and Scotti's father was standing in the kitchen talking to his wife. He had just returned from a flight and was still wearing his dark-blue pilot's uniform. Although not tall, he was an extremely handsome man with silver hair and deeply tanned skin. "Distinguished" was the best word to describe him, Lorna thought, distinguished the way an airline captain should be.

"Hello, Lorna," he said warmly. "Welcome to our house. Of course you're not a stranger, and we hope you'll be comfortable."

Lorna started to respond when she suddenly noticed that they were smiling at her. But that was not all. They were looking UP and smiling at her. Both of them. She felt like a giant because she was looking DOWN at her best friend's parents. She was accustomed to looking down at Mrs. Wheeler. After all, Scotti's mother was only five feet two inches tall. And she remembered that Scotti had mentioned sometime that pilots had to be at least five feet six and that her father had barely made the cutoff, but Lorna couldn't remember ever feeling that she towered over him before. She looked down at her shoes. Of course. That was it. She was wearing espadrilles with two-inch heels. That made her five feet nine to Captain Wheeler's five feet six.

Lurching forward into a gigantic slump, Lorna muttered "Thanks," hurried to Scotti's room, sat down on the edge of the bed, and stared at herself in the mirror. It was crazy, she thought, but somehow she had imagined that being the Wheelers' daughter for a while would actually make her shorter, or at least make her feel that way. Instead, the opposite was true. She felt more like a giraffe than ever.

Lorna gazed off into space thinking about her predicament and lost all track of time until a soft tap sounded at the door. "Lorna? Are you awake?"

"Sure, Mrs. Wheeler, I'm awake."

"Dinner's ready, sweetie. As soon as you're ready, we'll eat."

"Be right there," Lorna sighed and looked at herself in the mirror again. "I'm not being fair," she said to the image that looked back at her. "Mrs. Wheeler is being super, and she hasn't hassled me once. So what if I'm a little bit bigger than Scotti's parents? It's a lot better than being at home and constantly being told to stand up straight and to maximize my potential."

Her uneasiness gone, Lorna joined the Wheelers at the dinner table. "Gosh," she said, looking at the gorgeous dish in the center of the table. "You can't tell by looking that it isn't regular lasagna." Then she laughed nervously. Maybe that hadn't been the right thing to say, she thought.

If Mrs. Wheeler's feelings had been hurt by Lorna's comment, she didn't show it. "Dig in," she instructed, handing Lorna a large serving spoon. "Guests first."

"She's not a guest. She's our new daughter," said Captain Wheeler with a hearty laugh.

Lorna took a small helping of the lasagna and filled the rest of her plate with salad, which was covered, as usual, with fresh bean sprouts. The lasagna had a surprising flavor—different, but actually pretty good. She was becoming more relaxed by the minute, and she eagerly joined in the light conversation. Captain Wheeler talked about the flight he had just returned from, leaving Dallas-Fort Worth for Denver and then on to Seattle and back again, and how the sun had actually shone the entire time he was in Seattle.

Mrs. Wheeler mentioned her own flight schedule and then turned to Lorna and said, "See, I told you that you'd like my lasagna. It doesn't have to be junk food to taste good." She was thoughtful for a moment and then added slowly, "You know, I really believe that Scotti is stunting her growth by eating junk food when she has all this good nutritional food available. Why, just think, if she had been eating properly all these years, she might be as tall as you are, Lorna."

Lorna was thunderstruck. She stopped the fork

in midair that was headed for her mouth, staring first at Mrs. Wheeler and then at the fork loaded with vitamin-packed, nutritious vegetable lasagna and then back at Mrs. Wheeler again.

But it was Captain Wheeler who spoke next. "And did you know, Lorna, that it is a proven fact that better understanding of the importance of good nutrition by the general public has resulted over the years not only in healthier people but in bigger people as well? I'm sure that if you've ever visited a museum or an old house you've noticed how small the beds were. A hundred years ago people were much shorter."

Then Mrs. Wheeler chimed in again. "I'm sure that if Craig and I had had the nutritional advantages when we were younger that today's children have, we would be much bigger people. Don't you agree, dear?"

How can this be happening to me? Lorna wondered. I would give anything to be short like Scotti, but now, living with the Wheelers and forced to eat nothing but health food, I'll probably grow to be six feet tall before I can move back home.

7

Tiffany was still pouting when Scotti reached the kitchen a few minutes after her encounter with Skip in the hall. She crossed her arms over her chest, stamped her foot, and turned her back on Scotti to show her disdain. Scotti ignored the whole performance. She was still trying to regain her composure after coming face to face with a practically nude Skip. At first, she had wanted to run back to Lorna's room and hide, but she had known instinctively that once inside the safety of that room, she might never have the nerve to come out again.

"Can I help, Mrs. Markham?" she now asked, sniffing the delicious aroma of barbeque.

"Scotti, darlin', please call me 'A-yan,'" she said, pronouncing "Ann" in her thick Texas accent.

Oh, oh, thought Scotti. It would be hard enough to call her best friend's mother by her first name, but did she mean that she should be called "A-yan," the

43

exact way she said it herself, or would it be okay to call her "Ann," the way Scotti normally pronounced that name? "Sure," she said at last, deciding to postpone that decision until another time. "Do you want me to set the table?"

"Absolutely not! You just sit right down and make yourself comfortable. I'm fixing a barbequed brisket and potato salad and all the other Markham family favorites to celebrate your staying with us. It'll be a party supper all in your honor. How does that sound?"

Scotti thought she would die from happiness. No tofu. No bean sprouts. No poached fish. Just good, old-fashioned food like beef dripping in barbeque sauce and potato salad full of delicious, fattening potatoes and delicious, fattening mayonnaise.

"Ummm. It sounds heavenly," she purred.

Scotti sat down on the sofa just inside the den where she could watch the dinner preparations. This is the life, she thought. No hassles over helping in the kitchen or getting exercise. All she had to do was make herself comfortable and wait for the feast. Mrs. Markham was a wonderful mom. How could Lorna be so blind?

As if she had been summoned by Scotti's thoughts about her, Lorna popped in the backdoor.

"Hi, everybody," she said brightly. "I forgot something. Just ignore me. I'll be gone in a second." She waved to Scotti as she disappeared down the hallway heading for her room.

Scotti started to follow her and ask how things were going in Slender City, but changed her mind. She didn't really want to know. Besides, the sofa was so comfortable and the barbecue aroma so delicious. I'm probably gaining weight just smelling it, she thought with a giggle.

A moment later Lorna reappeared with her clock radio tucked under one arm. Tiffany ran to her sister, tackling her around the hips and burying her face in Lorna's stomach.

"Oh, Lorna. Please come home. I miss you! I miss you!" she cried, breaking out in loud, tearless sobs. Her eyes were closed tightly, but every few seconds she would open one a slit and look at Scotti, presumably to make sure Scotti was watching.

"Sure you do," said Lorna wriggling out of Tiffany's grip. "Wow, Mom. What smells so good?" she cried, but then she sighed and added in a deflated-sounding voice, "You're not having brisket, are you? You know that's my favorite."

"Of course we are, darlin'. We're having a special supper in honor of Scotti."

"You could stay if you wanted to," Scotti offered. She felt guilty at the miserable look on her best friend's face.

"That's okay," said Lorna. "Mrs. Wheeler is having a special supper for me, too. I'd better get back. It might be ready."

"Isn't that nice of her," Mrs. Markham drawled. "What is she fixing?"

Lorna looked as if she would love to dig a hole and crawl in it. "Vegetable lasagna," she said weakly. "It's very nutritious. Well, I'd better go now. Bye."

Scotti could barely swallow the laugh that was rising in her throat and threatening to burst from her lips. Of course, she really did feel sorry for Lorna, but vegetable lasagna! And for a celebration supper! It was one of the most gross things her mother fixed. She used slices of squash instead of noodles and thin, watery tomato juice instead of thick, luscious tomato paste. Poor Lorna! she thought. I hope she survives.

Just then Tiffany let out a shriek. "Daddy!" she cried as Coy Markham strode into the house. He tossed his cowboy hat onto the cattle horns mounted beside the backdoor and swung Tiffany over his head in what appeared to be one long, continuous motion.

"How's Daddy's little lady?" he asked kissing her on the cheek. Then he turned to Scotti and said, "And how's my new daughter? Is that brisket I smell? It looks like Mamma is going all out to welcome you to our house."

Scotti blushed, but before she could answer, Ann Markham turned and said, "Of course, I've gone all out. It isn't every day that we get a daughter as special as Scotti, and you'd better wash up because as soon as Skip gets in here we'll eat!"

Skip! Scotti's heart was racing. She had momentarily forgotten about him, and at the sound of his name, he appeared, looking unbearably handsome in jeans and a pale-blue polo shirt that set off his gorgeous tan. Scotti looked down instantly and began studying the pattern of the tile on the kitchen floor. There was no way she could look him in the eye. Not after she had seen him wearing nothing but a towel.

"Sit down, sit down," Mrs. Markham ordered. "And Scotti, darlin', you sit right here."

To Scotti's horror she pulled out the chair directly across from Skip and motioned for her to sit there. "Thanks," Scotti murmured as she slid into the chair without looking up.

For the next few moments everyone was too occupied with passing the meat platter, scooping helpings of potato salad and beans, and buttering hot rolls to pay much attention to Scotti. She took the dishes that were passed by Mr. Markham on her left and handed them to Mrs. Markham on her right while managing to keep her head down far enough to avoid Skip's gaze. With any luck at all she could stay this way all through dinner, even if it meant a stiff neck.

"Scotti, I've been telling Mr. Markham— whoops, I guess you'd better call him 'Coy' if you're going to call me 'A-yan.' Well, anyway, I've been telling him all about how you want to be a writer, and we both remember that WONDERFUL article you had published in our local paper. I think it's marvelous and he does, too. Don't you, darlin'?"

"That's right. It's a dog-eat-dog world out there, and it's never too early to get started."

Scotti swallowed her barbeque, trying not to think about dogs eating other dogs, and murmured a thank you. She wondered what Skip thought about the compliments his parents were paying her and hoped he was genuinely impressed. Maybe it would be a good idea to write an article about the Markham family, after all, she thought. Then she could actually interview Skip.

"And, of course, it's just marvelous that you have the foresight to know you want to be a foreign exchange student when you get to high school and to take steps to train yourself for it," said Mrs. Markham, bringing Scotti back to the present.

"Lorna wants to be one, too," said Scotti.

"Yes, but I'm sure it was your idea." Mrs. Markham shook her head sadly. "Lorna's biggest problem is that she doesn't plan ahead. But you know already that you want to be a writer and a foreign exchange student. Now that is what I call foresight."

"Scotti wants to be an astronaut. Don't you, Scotti?" piped up Tiffany.

Scotti looked up in surprise. "An astronaut?" she asked. "Where did you get an idea like that?"

"From Skippy. He said you wanted to be an astronaut, didn't he, Mom? He said you wanted to be an astronaut because you were so sp—"

"Knock if off, Tiff," Skip shouted gruffly. "You don't know what you're talking about."

Scotti felt lightheaded, as if the floor had opened up beneath her. Skip was coming to her rescue. Not only that—he must think she was pretty special if he had thought she wanted to become an astronaut.

"I do so too know what I'm talking about, Skip Markham," Tiffany insisted. "You said it. I heard you. You said that Scotti was—"

"TIFFANY!" her mother shouted. "Now that's enough." Then turning to Scotti, she added, "Here, darlin', have some more potato salad."

Scotti took another helping of the potato salad and nibbled at it, but suddenly she couldn't taste a thing. Could it possibly be true? Had Skip been talking about her to his family? Had he been complimenting her? Talking about how intelligent she was? Maybe he was starting to care for her the way she cared for him. And if she and Lorna hadn't traded places, she might never have suspected.

The rest of the evening was a blur, but finally the dishes were done and she was back in Lorna's room. She slipped into her nightgown and flipped the lock on the door so that Tiffany would not come barging in again. Then she pulled her notebook containing *Prisoner of Fate* from under her pillow, propped herself up in bed, and began to write:

> *The banquet to welcome Dianna to Markham Castle had been set out in the great hall.*

That isn't right, Scotti thought, and with a sigh she scratched it out. She stared into space for a few minutes and then started writing again.

> *"Your Ladyship, you have never looked more beautiful," said the handsome gentleman as he caressed her hand with his lips.*

*"Oh, thank you, Lord Markham," she
answered demurely.*

*"Please call me Skip," he said, drawing
her close to him. "And I'll call you Dianna."*

Scotti frowned again. This wasn't working at all.
There was something wrong. What was it? Finally she
pulled the spoiled sheet out of the notebook and
tossed it onto the floor. She smiled to herself as she
began writing across the top of a new page:

JOURNEY TO THE STARS

Chapter 1

8
_____

Lorna made it through the meal somehow, nibbling just enough of the food to be polite, but being careful at the same time not to eat any more than was absolutely necessary, in spite of Mrs. Wheeler's frequent suggestions that she take another helping of vegetable lasagna. When she was finally able to excuse herself and retreat to Scotti's room, Lorna was already beginning to formulate a plan. There was only one thing to do. She would have to find a way to counteract all the vitamins Mrs. Wheeler would be pushing at her. It was a matter of life or death. She would absolutely die if she grew any taller, so she would have to stunt her own growth. If Scotti could do it, surely she could, too.

Rummaging around in Scotti's desk, Lorna found a blank sheet of paper and a stubby pencil with the eraser chewed off. It would do, she thought resolutely. Then across the top of the page she wrote:

HOW TO STUNT MY GROWTH

Numbering to ten down the left side of the page, she stopped short of writing "junk food" beside number one. That takes in a lot of territory, she thought. Hamburgers were ground beef and that was perfectly good for you. And pizza was covered with cheese, which was from one of the five essential food groups she had studied in health class. But at the same time, wasn't Mrs. Wheeler always lecturing Scotti about chocolate and how it was a depressant? She meant that it affected Scotti's mood, of course, making her sad or crabby or both, but "depress" also meant to push down, which was the opposite of letting something grow up. Was it possible that eating a lot of chocolate would keep her from growing, too? It was worth a try, she decided, so beside number one she wrote "chocolate."

What other junk foods were there that could be added to her list? Lorna stared at the ceiling for a moment, visualizing the order counter at McDonald's. French fries! Why hadn't she thought of them before? They were greasy, covered with salt, and full of those terrible carbohydrates that Mrs. Wheeler avoided so strenuously. If that isn't enough to stunt a person's growth, I don't know what is, Lorna thought happily as she added French fries to her list.

Suddenly, she heard a voice echoing in her mind. It was her Grandmother Markham who had died the year before but was still very much alive in Lorna's memory. When she closed her eyes she could see Grandmother Markham shaking her old white head as she had so many times and pointing her finger as she lectured Lorna and her brother a few years ago. "Don't you take up drinking coffee. It'll stunt your growth!" Her mother had always chuckled over the old woman's warning, calling it an old wives' tale. But Lorna couldn't help remembering that her father was six feet two and he didn't drink coffee, but her grandmother had been shorter than most of the other members of the Markham family. She probably knew what she was talking about first hand, Lorna thought, and with a flourish of her pencil, coffee was number three.

She thought and thought for a while longer but could not come up with any more additions to her list. I suppose that three is enough for one evening, she decided. Folding the paper, she put it back into the desk drawer, but there was one more thing she wanted to do with the pencil.

Lorna glanced around Scotti's room. It was ultra-feminine, just the same as Scotti was, and each of the four walls was painted a different pastel color. The bedroom door was set into a sunny yellow wall, the closet into pale pink, the window into soft green, and the fourth wall, where Scotti's brass bed stood, was a baby blue. The four colors were picked up as stripes in the white ruffled curtains and bedspread, giving the room the look of perpetual springtime. Flowers bloomed and a large-eyed kitten looked out from posters on the wall, and a feathery asparagus fern hung in front of the window.

"Where can I put it so that it won't show?" Lorna wondered aloud. She finally decided on the corner where the pink and green walls met. It was more shadowy than the other corners since it was farthest away from the bedside lamp.

Slipping off her shoes, Lorna backed up against the pink side of the corner. She pulled herself up to her full height and ran one hand over the top of her head, placing the index finger against the wall. Then, grasping the pencil in the other hand, she made a short mark on the wall beside the spot marked by her finger. She stood back and looked at it with satisfaction. The mark barely showed. In fact, it was doubtful that anyone who didn't already know it was there would ever notice it, she thought.

Lorna breathed a sigh of relief. Now she would be able to check every day to see if her growth was spurting because of Mrs. Wheeler's nutritious cooking. Or, she thought with a sly smile, if I'm actually able to stunt my growth.

She awoke with a start the next morning. First, she was aware of the bright sunshine streaming through the windows and straight into her eyes. Then there was the insane pounding on the bedroom door.

"Who is it?" she called thickly.

"Lorna? It's me. Helene Wheeler," came a chirpy voice. "Rise and shine. It's an absolutely glorious day. Come and join me on the pool deck for some Jazzercise before we have breakfast."

Lorna scowled and rolled over toward her clock

radio. Shielding her eyes from the brightness, she saw with horror that it was only 6:45 A.M. What's wrong with that woman? she thought. It's practically the middle of the night. Not only that, it's Sunday. But aloud she said, "Be there pretty soon."

Turning her back to the window, she pulled the pillow over her head and tried to get comfortable again. She had no intention of jumping around on the pool deck at this hour. She had almost drifted back to sleep when the pounding started on her door once more.

"Come on, sack rat," Mrs. Wheeler called, a bit louder this time. "You don't want all that lasagna to go to your hips, now do you?"

"I'm coming! I'm coming!" It was obvious that she would get no peace until she gave in to her new mother.

Lorna dragged herself out of bed, pulled on jogging shorts and a tank top, and staggered out of the room. "This had better be the shortest Jazzercise routine in history," she grumbled half-aloud. She found Mrs. Wheeler prancing around on the pool deck, warming up in a workout suit of electric-green-and-orange graffiti print that was so bright it made Lorna squint. To make matters worse, Lorna's stomach had begun growling piteously.

Helene Wheeler grinned broadly and clicked a cassette into a portable tape player on the umbrella table. "Just watch me and do what I do," she instructed. "You'll catch on in no time."

At the same instant that the music blasted out of

the tape player, Mrs. Wheeler began to gyrate and hop around to the beat, thrusting her arms in every direction and raising each leg in a perfect kick.

"Jump in anywhere," she called to Lorna.

Lorna sighed and closed her eyes, thinking longingly of the Markham family tradition of sleeping late on weekends. Even Tiffany knew enough to stay quiet until nine by looking at the comics in the morning paper or playing in her room. Jazzercise at 6:45 in the morning! It was madness. That was all there was to it.

Aware that Mrs. Wheeler was probably watching her critically and was about to bark another round of orders, Lorna managed to bounce a little bit to the music and flop her arms around in various directions. If she could just get this over with and then get something to eat and go back to bed, she might survive.

"That's fine. You're doing great. Now pick up the tempo and get those feet off the ground. Kick! Kick! Kick!"

Okay. So I'll kick, Lorna thought with resignation. She drew back her right leg and thrust it forward into the air. At the same time she kicked, she felt a sharp pain in her foot as it struck something solid. Then she heard a loud splash. Opening her eyes, she saw in horror that what she had kicked was a bright-yellow webbed lawn chair and that it was now sinking into the deep end of the pool.

Mrs. Wheeler was standing with an astonished look on her face at the edge watching the lawn chair go down. "Well, you certainly do know how to kick," she said with a nervous little laugh.

Lorna was so embarrassed she thought she would die. The Wheelers all had short legs. They could probably do high kicks in the shower without touching the tile walls, but she was such an amazon that the lawn furniture wasn't safe when she lifted her foot anywhere in the backyard.

"I'll go in and get it in a little while," she promised as soon as she could find her voice.

"Don't you worry about it. It's perfectly fine right where it is for now," Mrs. Wheeler reassured her. "Whoever is the first one into the pool today will get to bring it out. Now let's go in and have some breakfast."

9

Scotti drifted slowly toward consciousness, wondering at first where she was. The digital readout on her bedside clock said 7:10 A.M., but where was the bright summer sun that usually streamed in through her window at this time of day? For an instant, she had the eerie feeling that she was locked inside a dark and silent tomb. But then she recognized the drapes pulled tightly across the window and the blue-flowered wallpaper, and she remembered where she was and why she was there. She was in Lorna Markham's room, and this was the Great Mom Swap.

Smiling with satisfaction, she crossed her arms behind her head and rocked until Lorna's water bed was in motion. Then she bobbed on the gentle waves and listened for sounds of activity from the Markhams. Surely, someone would be up by now. She was starved and anxious for breakfast. Pancakes, maybe, with creamy butter and thick maple syrup, or French toast dredged in powdered sugar. Or, she thought with mouth-watering anticipation, jelly donuts!

Being the Markhams' daughter was really the life. Maybe she and Lorna could make the switch permanent, or at the very least, maybe they would let her come for meals even after the girls moved back home. That idea appealed to Scotti most. After all, she did miss her own parents a little. But vegetable lasagna? Not at all.

Suddenly, a thought occurred to her that made her leap out of bed and into her bathrobe. The Markhams were probably all at the breakfast table, and they were being extra quiet so as not to disturb her. She could see the stack of pancakes dwindling, the last piece of French toast being whisked onto someone's plate, and not even a crumb left on the platter where the jelly donuts had been.

Scotti pressed her ear against the door, listening for the faint murmur of conversation. Nothing. Then she opened the door a crack and listened again. Still nothing. And there were no delicious aromas floating in the air, either. Was it possible that everyone was still asleep?

By this time, her stomach had gone far past mere pleading for breakfast; it was up to all-out insistence. She thought fleetingly about raiding the survival kit in the back of Lorna's closet but decided against it. Who knew when there might be a real emergency? Maybe I could sneak into the kitchen and make myself a couple of pieces of toast to tide me over until breakfast, she reasoned.

Satisfied with that idea, she slipped into the hall. The door to Ann and Coy's bedroom was tightly shut as she tiptoed past it, and Tiffany's door was only slightly ajar. So far, so good. But as she moved down the hall toward the kitchen, she could see that Skip's bedroom door was wide open, and she would have to go past it. Her heart started to pound as she reconsidered what she was doing. What if he was awake and saw her sneaking to the kitchen like a thief? Worse yet, she hadn't even combed her hair. Or washed her face. Or put on any lip gloss. She looked as rumpled as the bed she had just climbed out of.

Suddenly, the lion in her stomach let out a tremendous roar, shocking her so much that she propelled forward. She clutched her middle and put on the brakes, almost collapsing with relief when she came to a stop, but then almost dying when she realized that she stood in front of Skip's open door. Too petrified to move, she stared straight ahead and waited for the words she had heard twice before. "How's it going, kid?"

The seconds dragged by, but Scotti heard only the ticking of the grandfather clock in the living room. She had never realized how loud it sounded before. Slowly, blood began to flow through her body again and her lungs started pumping air again, too. He must be asleep. He hadn't seen her make an idiot of herself just because her stomach growled. She was safe, and she could go on to the kitchen to make some toast.

She started to inch forward again, but something held her back. Skip was the boy of her dreams. And he was probably starting to like her too, since he thought she was going to be an astronaut. Here was her chance to see him sleeping, to gaze at his handsome face and tousled hair without anybody ever knowing, just the way heroines sometimes did in romance novels. Closing her eyes, she slowly turned her head toward Skip's open door. The house was still completely silent as she gradually opened her eyes to a slit and gazed out through the fringes of lashes. There he was, lying face down with his head to one side. His handsome face looked so peaceful, and his breathing was slow and measured. Scotti's rapturous gaze traveled downward from his head to where his arms curved upward toward the head of the bed. Down to where the muscles of his shoulders and back glistened in the soft light. And on down to HIS JOCKEY SHORTS!

Oh my gosh! she thought, sucking in her breath. She turned her head away instantly and tore on down the hallway as fast as she could go on tiptoe. I SAW HIM IN HIS UNDERWEAR!

She was breathless and her pulse was racing when she sank into a chair at the kitchen table. The picture of Skip sprawled across his bed, covers thrown aside and wearing nothing but his underwear, rolled through her mind like a runaway movie. Thank goodness no one saw, she prayed silently over and over again, but how will I ever face him knowing that I've seen him that way?

Suddenly, Scotti wasn't hungry anymore, and the thought of swallowing toast—even toast with jelly on it—made her stomach roll. All she wanted was to get back to her bedroom before anyone got up and found her here. She could hide there and plan what she was going to do next.

The hallway back to the bedroom seemed five miles long. She held her breath and kept her eyes straight ahead when she went past Skip's open door. Finally, she thought as she streaked into the bedroom and sank against the door, closing it behind her. She had made it. She was safe.

"What does 'fate' mean?" said a tiny voice. "I know what 'prisoner' means, but what is 'fate'?"

Scotti lurched toward the desk where Tiffany sat with the ring binder open before her that contained both *Prisoner of Fate* and *Journey to the Stars* and snatched it up before Tiffany knew what was happening.

"What are you doing with that?" Scotti demanded. She tried to keep from speaking loudly enough to wake the family, so the words came out as a hoarse whisper. "Don't you know you're supposed to stay out of other people's property?"

Tiffany looked unimpressed. "So what does 'fate' mean?"

"It's all the terrible things that are going to happen to you if you ever come into this room again. Understand?"

"I can come in if I want to. It's my house, and this is my sister's room. So there."

"It *was* your sister's room, but now it's mine. And you had better leave my things alone or I'm going straight to your parents."

"Oh, no you won't." Tiffany wore a smug expression, but Scotti was too angry to care.

"Oh, yes I will. Watch me."

"Oh, no you won't, or I'll tell everybody that you were looking at Skippy in his underwear."

10

It was all Lorna could do to keep from wrinkling her nose at the brownish-colored drink that Helene Wheeler set before her.

"Drink it up. You'll love it," said Captain Wheeler. He was leaning forward across the kitchen table and watching her as if he were anticipating something wonderful. "What do you put in this, dear? Carrot juice, wheat germ? I can't remember."

Mrs. Wheeler must have seen the look on Lorna's face because she only shrugged and said, "That's my little secret. All I'll tell you is that it's packed with vitamins and will give you more energy than you'll know what to do with."

Lorna looked around the room helplessly. Why wasn't Tiffany here, spilling something and distracting everybody long enough for Lorna to pour this disgusting stuff down the drain? It was terrible being an only child. There was nowhere to escape, no one else to blame things on. It's as if I'm on some kind of stage, she thought, a star, and everybody is watching my every move.

As if on cue, Mrs. Wheeler took her place at the table and joined her husband in staring at Lorna. "Go on. Try it. I promise you'll like it."

Trapped, thought Lorna, as she looked back at the glass sitting in front of her. Had it gotten bigger? Lorna blinked and looked at it again, certain that it was almost twice the size it had been a moment ago. She was horror-stricken. If it does that to a glass, what will it do to me? I'll grow a quarter of an inch before lunch.

"Relax," said Mrs. Wheeler. She put a reassuring hand on Lorna's. "There's not a drop of carrot juice in the drink I've made this morning. It gets its color from herb tea and honey. But that's all I'm going to tell you. You'll have to taste it to find out what else is in it."

This is one persistent woman, thought Lorna, knowing she would never get out of drinking it, no matter how disgusting it turned out to be. Slowly, she raised the glass to her lips and was just about to take the world's smallest sip when sounds from the patio caught her attention.

"Good morning, everybody." It was Scotti, and she hurried in the backdoor as if she were being chased. "I just came over to get my records." She whisked on through the house toward her room without stopping, but not before she managed to raise an eyebrow at Lorna. That meant she wanted Lorna to follow her. It was their secret signal.

Lorna scrambled to her feet. "I need to talk to Scotti about something," she said. Then with a stab of conscience she added, "But save this for me. I love tea and honey. I'll drink it in a few minutes."

She wasted no time getting to Scotti's room, where her petite friend was pacing the floor in an obvious fit of rage.

"I'm going to kill that monstrous little sister of yours!"

Lorna couldn't help but smile. "What has she done now?"

Scotti shrugged in exasperation. "Everything. The brat," she sputtered. "She snuck into my room while I wasn't there and was actually trying to read *Prisoner of Fate*. Did you know that little monster can read? She's only six."

"Of course I knew she could read. She started reading when she was four. Wait until my mom starts raving about that. 'Tiffany is so precocious. And so bright. There's no doubt that she'll maximize her potential when she gets older,'" mimicked Lorna. "I hear almost as much about Tiffany reading as I do about that one lousy article you had published in the newspaper."

"Well, besides snooping around in my things, she spies on me, too."

"Ooooh," cooed Lorna. "And tell me, what wicked and sinful things did she catch you doing?"

Scotti colored slightly. "Nothing," she insisted. "I didn't do anything wicked and sinful, as you put it. I just don't like to be spied on."

Lorna shook her head. "Tiffany must have something on you to shake you up this much."

"It's just that I'm used to my privacy."

She was interrupted by a sharp knock at the door. "Scotti," called her mother. "Mrs. Markham just called. Breakfast is ready, and they're waiting for you."

Scotti sighed helplessly. "I have to go now, but let's get together this afternoon. You have to help me figure out what to do about Tiffany."

"You can come over for a swim if you'll bring me something yummy, like a cinnamon roll or a piece of cake."

At first Scotti seemed startled at the idea of being invited to her own swimming pool, but then her expression turned to sympathy and she said, "Sure. I'll bring everything I can find. I know what you're going through."

Lorna followed her friend back to the kitchen where Mrs. Wheeler waited for them at the breakfast table.

"Now, Scotti," she began before either of the girls or Scotti's father could get in a word. "I just hope that you're behaving yourself over there and being polite and offering to help every way you can."

"Mom! You don't have to worry. I'm not some social pervert, you know."

"Of course not, dear. But you do tend to be a bit lazy when it comes to helping out, and you know how you overeat. That can be very bad manners."

"Come on, Helene," Captain Wheeler interjected. "Scotti will remember her manners. Won't you, dear?"

Scotti bit her upper lip and raised her eyes to the ceiling as if to pray for strength. "Mom," she insisted, "I said you don't have to worry. I won't do anything to embarrass you or Dad. Now I have to go. They're waiting for me."

Mrs. Wheeler's mood changed abruptly as if expressing her concern had made everything all right again. "Bye, dear. Have a wonderful time."

"Bye, Mom. Bye, Dad." Giving her father a peck on his upturned cheek, she threw Lorna a helpless look and hurried out the backdoor.

Lorna felt suddenly as if she were on center stage again. The kitchen had gotten completely quiet the instant Scotti left it, and all eyes were focused on her, waiting for her performance. It's my big moment, she thought. Lorna Markham, Broadway star and only child, will now drink her disgusting brown breakfast in front of a sellout crowd. Lorna lifted the glass to her lips and drained it in two gigantic gulps. Placing the glass on the table again, she said solemnly, "Thank you. It was very delicious." In her mind she could hear thunderous applause and see the standing ovation as rosebuds were tossed at her feet.

In reality, Mrs. Wheeler asked brightly, "Would you like another glass?"

It had gone down so quickly that Lorna had barely tasted it, and she thought a moment before answering. It hadn't been too bad, but then it hadn't been great either: sort of sweet, sort of yucky. "No, thanks. It really filled me up."

Lorna waited for someone to say something else, but no one did. Instead, both Wheelers continued to look straight at her, smiling faintly. Captain Wheeler had put down his newspaper to look at her, and Mrs. Wheeler reached for a slice of lemon, squeezed it into her tea, and began stirring without ever taking her eyes off Lorna's face. Oh, my gosh, Lorna thought. Drinking my breakfast was only the first act. They're waiting for me to do something else.

She racked her brain for something clever to say. What had she and Scotti's mother laughed about all those times? They had really broken up over practically nothing, but now her mind was blank as she sat there looking down at them and feeling ten feet tall and totally tongue-tied. It was the pits.

Finally, a single stray thought fluttered into her mind. "If you'll excuse me, I'd better brush my teeth."

In the sanctuary of the bathroom, Lorna dragged the toothbrush back and forth across her lower-left molars and pondered her situation. She stuck out like the proverbial sore thumb in this family of pygmies, and she was miserable. Not miserable enough to make her want to go back home and be hassled to death again, she thought, but miserable enough to work out a trade. She might even be willing to take Tiff off Scotti's hands for a while. She might, that is, for a price.

11

It was zero hour. Scotti left her own house and the unpleasant scene with her mother and trudged toward the Markhams', knowing that the time had come. She would have to face Skip at breakfast. There was no use wishing that he would sleep until noon and miss breakfast entirely. She knew better. Lorna always talked about the Markhams' Sunday breakfast and how it was a big family affair held in the dining room and how you had to have one foot in the grave to miss it.

Entering the kitchen, she deposited her records on the table beside the door and called out, "Hi. I'll wash my hands and be right there."

Above the splashing of the water she could hear the family talking among themselves. There could be no doubt that one of the voices belonged to Skip. She took a deep breath and hurried to the dining room where the good china and silver had been laid out on a pristine white tablecloth.

"G'mornin', darlin'," Mr. Markham called out.

"Good morning," she answered, heading for the one empty chair. "I hope I haven't kept everybody waiting."

"Nonsense," Ann drawled. "Now just help yourself to the scrambled eggs, the sausage, and the grits. The homemade cinnamon rolls will be out of the oven in a minute."

Scotti stared at the yellow rose in the center of her plate, trying to summon the courage to look up. Skip was sitting directly across from her again, and just knowing he was there made her tingle all over. She shuddered, wondering if she would ever be able to look at him again without remembering the way she had seen him earlier that morning.

"Here, little miss, help yourself to a good Texas breakfast." Coy Markham was holding an enormous platter just to Scotti's right. She nodded, grateful for some activity to take her mind off Skip, and began scooping scrambled eggs onto her plate. She took a sausage patty and then reached for the platter to pass it on to Tiffany.

"Hey, wait a minute," Skip said. It startled her so much that she almost dropped the platter. Was he talking to her?

Scotti looked up into Skip's dazzling blue eyes. He had been talking to her, all right, and he was actually smiling.

"Don't tell me that you aren't going to have some

grits. Just think how hurt Mamma will be. She makes the best grits in the state of Texas."

Scotti was pretty sure that he was teasing, but she looked hurriedly for Ann, who had gone back to the kitchen to get the cinnamon rolls. Now what was she going to do? Smiling shyly at Skip, she looked back at the dreaded grits lying in a sickly white lump on the platter. She knew that they were considered special in this part of the country. But she had tried them once, just after her family had moved to Texas four years before, and they had tasted disgusting. So disgusting that she had avoided them ever since.

But this was different. Skip was talking to her. Actually saying more than "How's it going, kid?" He was inviting her to try one of his family's favorite foods. Not only that, he wasn't about to let her off the hook.

"I think that we ought to initiate this little Yankee girl into the wonderful world of grits. Don't you, Dad?"

Coy Markham grinned and picked up the joke. "Why that's a fine idea, Son. Just help yourself to a big spoonful, Scotti. Then cover them with butter and salt and pepper and ummm, ummm!"

"Boys! Are you teasing this poor child?" Ann Markham had come back into the room carrying a steaming pan of delicious-smelling cinnamon rolls.

"It's okay," Scotti assured her. "I was going to try them anyway."

Scotti took a small helping of grits and passed the platter on. Her face was burning from the thrill of having Skip talk directly to her, and she was sure that it was noticeably red. But aside from that, this breakfast was going astonishingly well.

Everyone grew silent as the rolls were passed and serious eating got underway. The cinnamon rolls were delicious, and Scotti soon discovered that, by putting a small bite of grits into her mouth with the roll, she could barely detect the disgusting taste of the grits.

As the meal drew to a close, Mrs. Markham started the conversation again. "I know I've said this before, Scotti, but I just can't get over how hard you work at your writing. You are really a fine example of someone who maximizes her potential."

Mrs. Markham paused to take a bite of her grits, and Scotti felt a glow spread over her from the woman's praise.

"Why, Tiffany was telling me just this morning how you let her read something you're working on right now. *Prisoner of Fate?* Did she say that's what it's called? I just think it's wonderful that you are willing to let our little girl read your story."

Scotti nearly choked on a bite of cinnamon roll and grits. So that was why Tiffany had been quiet all through the meal. She knew that her mother could never resist talking about people who maximized their potential.

She shot a quick look at Tiffany, who smiled innocently at her, and then shoved half a sausage patty into her mouth wishing she could wring that scrawny little neck. That monster, she thought. She knows that she can talk about my book to her heart's content because if I try to shut her up she'll make good on her threat to tell that I saw Skip in his underwear. Well, I'll show her. I'll talk about my writing, too.

Scotti smiled triumphantly at Tiffany and then turned to her parents. "Gee, I'm glad you're interested. I'm writing a novel. I've been working on it for almost a year, and just recently I started another one called *Journey to the Stars*. It's all about some astronauts."

From across the table came a low whistle of approval. "Novels, huh?" said Skip. "That's really something."

"I'd say that it is," said Mrs. Markham. "It just goes to show what a person can do if she really wants to. Now you take Tiffany. She's been reading since she was four. That child is going to amount to something someday."

Mrs. Markham droned on about Tiffany's marvelous reading skills, but Scotti scarcely heard. She was off on another cloud of rapture because of Skip's reaction to her writing. He really was getting interested in her, and it might never have happened without the Great Mom Swap. Suddenly, she was aware that all eyes were upon her. Startled, she looked around questioningly.

"Didn't you hear my question, darlin'?" Ann asked. "I said, would you like to hear Tiffy read for you?"

"Sure."

"Whoopee!" shouted Tiffany. "You don't have to get a book, Mamma. I've already got something right here."

She whipped a sheet of notebook paper out of her lap and began to read, sounding out the bigger words as she went. "Jour- . . . journey to the Stars. . . . Chapter 1. Dianna trumb- . . . no . . . tremb- . . . trembled as her true love . . . raced to meet her in the moon . . . light."

Scotti went numb. She felt as if her body had disappeared and only her face, which was burning red from embarrassment, remained. But still, she knew that her body couldn't be gone because her pulse was pounding loudly in her ears.

"He swept her into his arms and KISSED her heh heh tenderly as"

"Tiffany! That's enough reading for today," Scotti shouted. Then, trying to regain her composure, she added, "It isn't ready to be read out loud yet. I haven't finished it or anything."

"But I was just getting to the good part."

Mrs. Markham cleared her throat in obvious embarrassment. "Now, Tiffy. That was lovely reading, and I'm sure Scotti is very impressed, but you'd best give her story back to her now."

Across the table, Skip shuffled uncomfortably. "May I be excused?" An instant later, he was gone from the room, and Tiffany's eyes sparkled mischievously as she handed the notebook paper to Scotti. That little monster, Scotti thought. I'll kill her yet.

12

It had not been difficult for Lorna to work out a trade with Scotti as they sunbathed beside the Wheelers' pool that afternoon.

"How would you like for me to take Tiffany off your hands all day tomorrow?" Lorna asked, trying to sound as casual as possible.

"What do you mean, take Tiffany off my hands?" Scotti asked. She raised herself up off the beach towel only to sink back again as Lorna reminded her that she was supposed to baby-sit Tiffany on days when Mrs. Markham worked for Office Temps.

"It was part of the switch, remember?"

"Oh, GROAN!" Scotti wailed. "You bet you can take her off my hands. Her life wouldn't be worth much with me."

"Good. I have a plan. Here's all you have to do to repay me for this gigantic favor."

* * *

The next morning was Monday, and Lorna headed for her own house to bring Tiffany back for the day. She was feeling especially good. Mrs. Wheeler had served a fantastic breakfast of strawberries, sliced bananas, chunks of fresh pineapple, and whole-bran muffins that had actually tasted great. Except for the nagging fear that all those vitamins would speed up her growth, Lorna had enjoyed the meal and had actually exchanged a few laughs with Mrs. Wheeler like they used to do in the old days. Now, if her plan worked and Scotti came through on her end of the bargain, she might just have solved the problem of how to live comfortably with the Wheelers and keep from outdistancing a giant redwood at the same time. If that happened, the Great Mom Swap would be a gigantic success.

Lorna's good mood was not destined to last long. Her mother was waiting for her at the backdoor. She swooped down on her so quickly that Lorna barely had time to notice that both Scotti and Tiffany were still at the breakfast table. Scotti was attacking a large stack of pancakes while Tiffany played in a dish of soggy cereal.

"Lorna Markham, what on earth were you thinking when you insisted to Scotti that you take care of Tiffany while I'm at work today? You know that I like for her to be cared for in her own home. The telephone number where I can be reached in an emergency is here. The doctor's number is here and the police and the fire department. And above all, you know that I don't like for her to be around a swimming pool unless I'm there to supervise."

Oh, boy, Lorna thought. Try to do a favor and what does it get you? Aloud she said, "Mom, Scotti needs some time to work on her writing. You know, to maximize her potential? I'm surprised you didn't think of it yourself. Besides, Tiffy wouldn't drown even if I weighted her feet with bricks. You know that she swims like a fish."

"Mamma! Mamma! Don't let her tie bricks to my feet," shouted Tiffany while Scotti gave Lorna a victory sign behind Mrs. Markham's back.

"Oh, my! What a terrible thought."

"Mom," Lorna protested. "It was just an illustration. You know that. Besides, I promise never to take my eyes off her. I'll stay glued to her all day long."

"Well," Mrs. Markham said slowly. "I can't imagine why you have this sudden interest in taking care of your little sister, but if you promise to behave responsibly—"

"I promise, I promise. Come on, Tiff. Get your fingers out of the cereal. I'll give you a banana at the Wheelers, and you can pretend you're a monkey."

Her mother was still staring openmouthed as Lorna half-dragged her little sister out the door. She expected to find the house deserted when she returned since Mrs. Wheeler had mentioned at breakfast that she would be out most of the day. Instead, Captain Wheeler was standing in the center of the den floor staring at the flickering television set. Looking up, he gave her a small wave.

"Aren't you going to work?" she blurted before she remembered that since he was an airline pilot he was home lots more than most fathers.

"Not if this is Monday. I'm flying Tuesday, Wednesday, and Thursday this week. It's a funny thing, though. My schedule is so crazy that I'm seldom sure what day of the week it is. I have to turn on the television to the Today Show every morning just to find out."

Lorna shook her head. Scotti had told her about this, but she had thought her best friend was putting her on. Nobody's father was home four days out of the week, although she did remember seeing Captain Wheeler around a lot when she had been visiting Scotti. This new development was going to change her plans for the day. She would have to alert Scotti. She barely heard Tiffany launch into the American Airlines commercial—"We're American Airlines, doing what we do BEST!"—as she slipped into the kitchen and dialed her own number on the phone.

"Is being a pilot lots of fun?" she heard Tiffy inquire.

Great, she thought. Tiffany could ask a million questions, which would give her the time she needed.

Scotti answered after the third ring.

"Is Mom gone?" asked Lorna.

"She just left. I was getting ready to come over."

"Hold up," cautioned Lorna. "Your dad's home today. He says he flies Tuesday, Wednesday, and Thursday this week. And did you know that he has to watch television every morning to find out what day it is?"

Scotti chuckled. "He also says that he hates being a pilot because there's too much yard work. Has he told you that one yet? It's his favorite. But anyway, back to the plan. Leave everything to me. I'll be over in about fifteen minutes."

Lorna hung up, hoping that Scotti knew what she was doing, and went to find Tiff. After all, she had promised her mother not to let her out of her sight. She found her little sister watching cartoons in the den. Captain Wheeler was nowhere to be seen. "So where's Captain Wheeler? Did he tell you all about being a pilot?"

"Yup," said Tiffany importantly. "He says he hates it because there's too much yard work. I think he had to go mow the lawn."

As if on cue, a lawnmower roared to life somewhere near the front of the house. Lorna sighed and sank back on the sofa beside Tiffany as the cartoon show blared away on the television. Maybe things weren't going so badly after all, she thought.

A few minutes later Lorna glanced out the window to see her petite friend, looking like a tiny blond thief, slip into the yard with a bulging blue pillowcase over her left shoulder.

When Scotti reached the backdoor, she stuck her head in and called, "Lorna, are you here? I brought over some things I found in your room that I thought you might need."

Lorna rushed to meet her. "It's okay. He's mowing the front lawn." Then she glanced back at Tiffany, who seemed too absorbed in Scooby Doo to have noticed Scotti's appearance, and added, "Come on. Bring it back to the bedroom."

Lorna had cleared a space on the closet floor where she hoped her supplies would be safe, and she began hastily unpacking the pillowcase and arranging them in neat rows.

Scotti looked on with a puzzled frown. "Chocolate cocoa? Canned shoestring potatoes? Instant coffee? Semisweet chocolate squares? Presweetened cereal? Dill pickles? Boy, Lorna, I sneaked all of it out of your mom's pantry like you said to do. I expected my mom's cooking to get to you, but what's all this stuff for, anyway? It makes one crazy survival kit."

"You know how your mother is always saying that you stunted your growth with too much junk food, Scotti?"

"Yes, but that's a lot of baloney. She and my dad are both short. Just think how strange I'd look in this family if I were tall."

Lorna pretended not to hear Scotti's negative opinion, since she had now formed her own opinions on the subject. Besides, how could Scotti know how awful it was to be so tall and how desperately she wanted to be short? "Well," she said with a broad sweep of her hand, "this is my junk food. If it can work for you, it can work for me. I'm going to load up on this stuff before each meal. That way I'll be too full for all that nutritious stuff that will make me grow even taller. Brilliant, don't you think?"

Scotti gave her an incredulous look. "I think my mother is actually getting to you with all her sermons about nutrition. No. It's worse than that. I wondered about your sanity when you offered to take Tiffany for the day, but now I'm convinced. You've flipped."

13

As soon as Scotti had deposited Lorna's supplies and had gone, Lorna got out a coloring book and crayons. She had brought them along to keep Tiffany entertained while she took care of more important projects such as stunting her growth—no matter how crazy Scotti thought the idea was.

Obediently, Tiffany climbed up onto one of the stools at the kitchen counter and began flipping through the coloring book and frowning.

"What's the matter?" asked Lorna. "Can't you find a picture you like?"

Tiffany shook her head. "I'm looking for a picture of an airplane."

"Sorry, but you're out of luck. This coloring book is all baby animals. Here. Look at this cute baby deer. A baby deer is called a fawn. Why don't you color him?"

Tiffany gave her sister a sour look. "I know that a

baby deer is called a fawn, and I want to color an airplane because I'm going to be a pilot when I grow up, just like Captain Wheeler."

"But I thought Captain Wheeler said he didn't like being a pilot because of all the yard work. Besides, I thought you wanted to be a lawyer."

Tiffany sighed as if her older sister's stupidity was really getting to her. "I am going to have a husband to do the yard work, and I'll have plenty of time to be a pilot AND a lawyer. In fact, that's where I'll get my lawyer customers—on the plane. After I take off, I'll walk down the aisle and see who needs a lawyer and then I'll SUE!"

Lorna chuckled. "Don't forget to land. And they're called clients, not lawyer customers."

"Okay. Okay. I'll get my clients and then I'll sue and then I'll land."

Tiffany seemed pleased with her logic, and she picked up a yellow crayon and began shading in a baby chick. Lorna tiptoed out of the kitchen thinking that her mother was probably right. Ann Markham went on day and night about how Tiffany was going to make something of herself someday and how wonderful it was that she had such big goals. Lorna felt miffed, as usual. She certainly had a big goal—to be short. And she had even worked out a plan to stunt her growth. Why couldn't her mother ever take her goals seriously?

She had sneaked a mug out of the kitchen cabinet earlier, and now she slipped a spoon into the pocket of her shorts. Listening for a moment to make certain that Captain Wheeler was still mowing the front yard, she grabbed the jar of instant coffee off the closet floor in Scotti's bedroom and hurried to the bathroom. She turned on the hot-water tap and read the directions on the side of the jar while the water heated. "Place one heaping teaspoon of coffee in cup and add eight ounces of boiling water."

She couldn't risk boiling water in the kitchen. Captain Wheeler might come in and ask what she was doing. Hot water from the bathroom faucet would have to do. Lorna stuck her finger into the stream of lukewarm water and looked at herself in the mirror. She studied herself closely. There was no doubt about it. She was getting taller. She turned and gazed sharply at the flowers in the wallpaper. She was sure that yesterday the little lavender one had been completely visible above her head, but today it barely showed at all.

She looked at the directions on the coffee jar again. One heaping teaspoon? At that rate it might take days or even weeks to have any effect. Smiling, Lorna shoveled three heaping teaspoons of coffee into the mug and added another half for good measure.

The water was hot now. She filled the cup and stirred down the little islands of granules that bobbed to the surface and floated around the rim. Finally, when the last of the coffee had dissolved, Lorna put the mug to her lips and took a sip.

"Oh, YUK!" She forced herself to swallow and then looked down into the almost black liquid in the cup. It was gross! Totally disgusting! But it was necessary. Nobody ever said that stunting your growth would be easy.

As she started to take another sip, she remembered the chocolate in her closet. It was only semisweet, the kind her mother used in baking, but it might cut the bitter taste of the coffee a little bit. She opened the bathroom door a crack and listened. All was quiet. She flipped off the light, slid into Scotti's bedroom, and dove for the chocolate cube on the closet floor. She shaved off a few strips with her spoon and watched them melt into puddles of brown on top of the darker liquid.

Squaring her shoulders, she raised the mug to her lips. "Chugalug!" she muttered and poured the coffee into her mouth and swallowed, not stopping until the mug was drained. The disgusting, bitter liquid was so overpowering that she collapsed on the floor and rolled onto her stomach.

An instant later she heard the bedroom door burst open. "Lorna! Are you dead?"

Tiffany's small hands shook her shoulder. "Yes, I'm dead," mumbled Lorna. "Go away and leave me in peace."

Tiffany shook her shoulder even harder. "If you aren't dead, then get up and find me some cookies. I'm hungry."

"I told you. I'm dead," said Lorna. She shut her eyes tightly, hoping that Tiff would take the hint and go away. She was certain that if she sat up the entire cup of black coffee would come up and spew all over Scotti's gorgeous pastel room.

But Tiffany did not go away. Instead, she straddled Lorna and began pounding on her back. "Come on, Lorna. I'm hungry. I've gotta have some cookies."

Lorna came up off the floor, spilling her little sister onto the carpet. Glaring down at her, she said, "The Wheelers don't have any cookies. You're out of luck."

"Yes, they do."

"No, they don't. They don't believe in cookies. But if you're really hungry I can get you some mushrooms or bean sprouts. Or how about a glass of carrot juice?"

Now it was Tiffany's turn to make a face. "Carrot juice?" she whispered. Frowning, she added, "But you said I could have a banana. You said so when we were still at our house. You promised."

"So I did," said Lorna, smiling to herself at the bit of child psychology she had just learned. "Let's go out into the kitchen and see if we can find you a banana."

A banana didn't sound bad to Lorna either, even though she knew that it was probably nutritious. It might take away the coffee taste that lingered in her mouth.

Lorna had just reached into the basket that hung above the kitchen sink and was about to pull out two beautiful bananas when the door from the garage flew open and Helene Wheeler raced inside, her face aglow.

"Hi, girls," she said breathlessly. "Oh, Lorna, where's your fath—I mean where's Captain Wheeler? I have to talk to him right away. It's important."

"He was mowing the front lawn a few minutes ago," offered Lorna.

"Well, he's not there anymore," Tiffany said importantly. "He's out back now, doing something to the roses."

"Great," said Mrs. Wheeler. She zoomed toward the backdoor but stopped when she got there and turned around. "Don't eat anything now, girls. Eating between meals isn't good for you. Besides, I've made a wonderful oriental chicken salad for our lunch. It's full of chicken and pea pods and tofu and bean sprouts, but first I have to talk to Captain Wheeler."

Lorna watched her speed out the door and wondered what could be so important. She certainly seemed happy about it, whatever it was.

She felt a tug at her shorts. "Do I have to eat lunch here?" Tiffany looked up at her with pleading eyes. "I don't like armyental chicken salad."

"You don't know that you don't like it. You've never eaten it," said Lorna, realizing at once that she sounded just like her mother. She started to correct Tiffany and tell her that it was "oriental" instead of "armyental" when a new scheme occurred to her. "Besides, if you're going to join the army, you'd better learn to like armyental chicken salad. They eat it all the time."

The Wheelers returned a few minutes later, and Captain Wheeler's grin was at least as big as his wife's.

"Don't tell Lorna yet," he cautioned. "I have to make a call first."

"Don't tell me what?" Lorna couldn't help but ask.

Helene Wheeler grinned slyly. "You'll find out in a minute. And keep your fingers crossed. If it works out the way we are hoping, you're going to love it."

Lorna fidgeted nervously as she watched Mrs. Wheeler scoop the chicken salad into lettuce cups as she hummed happily. She could hear Captain Wheeler talking on the phone in the next room, but she could not make out what he was saying. After what seemed like an hour, he came back into the kitchen. "It's all set," he said happily. "The three of us are going to Hawaii."

Lorna felt her mouth drop open, but she was powerless to do anything about it. "Hawaii?" she whispered.

"Sit down and I'll explain the whole thing," said Mrs. Wheeler as she motioned toward the table where lunch was waiting. "I ran into Marci Wright at the dentist this morning. Her husband is a pilot, too, and he has enough seniority that he gets the Hawaii run every weekend. He flies out on Friday morning and returns home Sunday morning after an all-night flight. Well, she said that Pete—that's her husband—and the entire crew picked up some kind of flu bug this past weekend, and the doctor says none of them will be ready to fly again by Friday. That means that someone else"—she paused, gesturing toward her husband—"has to pilot the plane and someone

else"—she paused again, gesturing toward herself—
"has to stand in for one of the flight attendants. And
that means YOU"—she paused a third time, and this
time she gestured toward Lorna—"get to come along
on one of our passes. Isn't it wonderful? Now you'll
get to see what it's really like to be part of an airline
family."

Scotti's father held up a cautionary hand. "Of
course, we won't be able to stay any longer than the
normal turnaround for a flight crew. Unfortunately,
Helene and I will be on the job instead of on vacation.
But," he added with a smile, "we'll have free time
while we're in Honolulu, and it should be a fun trip for
you anyway."

All Lorna could do was grin. Hawaii! She was
actually going to Hawaii. Mrs. Wheeler had set the
whole thing up. She had to be the greatest mom in
the world.

14

On Monday morning the Markham house was finally peaceful enough for Scotti to get some serious writing done. Mr. Markham had a job like most fathers and had left shortly after eight for the bank where he was a vice president. Skip was working construction for the summer and had gone much earlier, since he had to be on the site by seven. That was good news to Scotti, since she did not want a repeat of Sunday morning's fiasco. Good news, too, was that Tiff the Terrible was spending the day with Lorna, and Mrs. Markham had gone on a job for Office Temps. It had never before occurred to Scotti just how exhausting so much family activity could be.

How could a writer possibly get any work done, she wondered, with people popping in and out all the time, with Tiffany spying and sneaking around where she didn't belong, and even with Skip—gorgeous,

fabulous Skip—rocking the house off its very founda-
tion with his stereo night and day?

She poured herself a glass of fruit punch,
scooped a handful of homemade chocolate chip
cookies out of the cookie jar, which, like practically
everything in the house, was shaped like the state of
Texas, and settled onto the sofa in the den. She had
decided to keep her ring binder hidden in her laundry
bag where Tiffany couldn't find it, so it smelled faintly
of dirty socks as she opened it to *Journey to the
Stars.*

This is going to be a great story, she thought. All
about Skip and me, two astronauts who fall deeply in
love as we journey through the romantic, star-
studded universe. Maybe she would even have an
eccentric scientist aboard the space ship who was
hoping to make a breakthrough in the area of stunting
people's growth. No, she decided. Who needs it? Besides, Scotti thought, Lorna had to be slightly wacko
if she honestly thought eating junk food would stunt
her growth. This was too serious a story to include
stuff like that.

She lay back against the sofa, closed her eyes,
and tried to picture Skip dressed in an astronaut's
jumpsuit like the ones she always saw on television.
But try as she might, she could not see him without
the cowboy hat that was always perched on one side
of his head.

She was jarred back to reality by the sound of the
telephone. Scowling, Scotti slid the notebook off her
lap and reached for the phone.

"Markhams," she said.

"Scotti? It's me. Ann. I'm so glad you're there, darlin'. I just read the most exciting thing in the morning paper. I would never have seen it myself, but one of the permanent girls in this department was showing the advertisement around and saying that she was going to do it. Oh, Scotti, I think it's wonderful. It could be your big chance. And to think that I, Ann Markham, will have been a part of it!"

"A part of what?" asked Scotti. She wasn't getting a thing out of what Ann was saying. It didn't make the least bit of sense.

"I'm not going to tell you. I'm going to let you read it for yourself. It's on page twenty-seven B in the bottom right-hand corner. Have to run now. And, Scotti, I just think it's soooo exciting!"

The morning newspaper was still scattered on the kitchen table along with the remnants of breakfast, including a pool of syrup on the plate where her pancakes had been, and Tiffany's uneaten cereal. Scotti grabbed the paper, tossing section after section back onto the table until she found the one she wanted, section B. Opening it to page 27, she read with astonishment the advertisement in the lower left-hand corner.

BOOK MANUSCRIPTS WANTED

Representative of a New York publisher
Will be reading manuscripts and interviewing
authors
At the Amfac Hotel at the Dallas-Fort Worth Airport

Friday, June 19, from 8 A.M. to 5 P.M.
Call (817) 571-7014 for an appointment

Scotti read through the ad four times before she realized that she was holding her breath. It was just too wonderful to be true. Lorna's mother had to be the most fabulous mom in the world. *Not only does she think it's great that I want to be a writer,* Scotti thought, *not like another mother I could mention. But she wants me to get my books published and even wants to help me do it.*

Scotti shot up straight as a pencil. The advertisement said that the representative of the New York publisher would be reading manuscripts and interviewing authors on June 19. That was this Friday, and it was only four days away. She grabbed her notebook again and turned to *Journey to the Stars*. It was going to be the greatest story of her career since it was about herself and Skip, but she could never have it ready to show a publisher's representative by Friday because it was only four pages long.

She would have to go with *Prisoner of Fate,* she decided. She had been working on it for almost a year, and the last entry she had written had been page 183, where Maude the Tyrant was sobbing on the fainting couch.

Scotti paused. There were a lot of similarities between Dianna's mother, Maude, and her own mother, but sobbing on the fainting couch certainly wasn't one of them. Helene Wheeler had been practically overjoyed when her daughter moved out.

Hadn't she even said that she thought the switch was a good idea? But Ann Markham had welcomed her with open arms, had thought it was wonderful that she was maximizing her potential to become a writer, and now THIS! It was too good to be true, and it was all because of the Great Mom Swap.

Scotti spent the rest of the day pouring over *Prisoner of Fate,* thinking several times that she had forgotten what a good story it was. Dianna was so beautiful and yet so tragic, and over and over again Scotti had to struggle to hold back tears. She took only one break, and that was to eat lunch and clean up the breakfast dishes. By late afternoon she had written the happy ending where beautiful Dianna had left the clutches of Maude the Tyrant forever and had gone to live happily ever after with her true love in Markham Castle.

She had scarcely written "The End" when Tiffany came bursting in the backdoor.

"It can't be that late already," Scotti muttered, but it was. The clock said four o'clock, which was as late as Lorna had agreed to keep Tiff out of her hair.

"Hi, Tiff," she said with a heavy sigh.

Doing a gigantic belly flop, Tiffany landed on the sofa beside Scotti, her face bright with excitement.

"Boy, is Lorna lucky. I want to live at your house so that I can be lucky, too."

"What are you talking about?" Scotti asked. "L ing at my house is no big deal."

"It is too! Your parents are flying to Hawaii this Friday, and Lorna gets to go along."

Scotti's heart stopped. "What did you say?" she demanded.

For once Tiffany looked frightened. Scotti tried to feel sorry for her, but the word "Hawaii" was ringing in her ears.

"Well!"

"Your parents are flying to Hawaii this weekend because someone named Pete got sick and can't go. They said Lorna could come along to see what it's really like to be in an airline family. I sure wish I could be in an airline family. Have you ever been to Hawaii, Scotti?"

Scotti nodded. "Once," she mumbled, "a long time ago."

It was true. Scotti had to admit to herself she had been to Hawaii once, a long time ago. And she had been to Acapulco and Cancun and New Orleans and even Disney World, and all because her parents worked for the airline and got passes. But still, she reasoned, she didn't get to go all that often, and taking Lorna somewhere like Hawaii was not only over-doing this mom-swap business, but it definitely wasn't fair. And to make matters worse, they were leaving on Friday. Even if they asked her to come along, she couldn't. Not on Friday. That was the day she was showing her novel to the New York publisher.

15

HAWAII. HAWAII. HAWAII. The word kept echoing in Scotti's mind long after Tiffany had run off to play. She picked up her novel, scarcely aware that she was doing it, and stomped off toward Lorna's room where she threw herself across the bed and stared at the bluebonnets in the wallpaper. Her parents were really going to take Lorna to Hawaii. Slowly, it began to make sense to Scotti. Hadn't her own mother called Lorna her "replacement" the morning the two of them had changed places? She had realized all along that her mother had thought the mom swap was a great idea. But there was more to it than that. She could see it clearly now.

She had believed that the mom swap was her own idea, that she had thought it up all by herself. But she could see now that it had been the work of her mother all along. My own mother wanted to get rid of me, she reasoned. She likes Lorna better because she's thin and says funny things like "mushing the mincerooms."

Scotti rolled over onto her back and studied the ceiling. But how did she manage it? she wondered. Did she drop really subtle hints at the dinner table? No! I have it, she thought, sitting up abruptly. She did it with subliminal suggestion.

Scotti tried to remember what she knew about subliminal suggestion. They had learned about it in a social studies unit on shoplifting. Supposedly, some department stores played music over their loud-speakers for shoppers to listen to, and there were messages such as "Don't steal!" and "Shoplifting is wrong!" hidden in the music. The words were so soft that people couldn't hear them with their ears. Instead, their subconscious minds heard the messages and obeyed them.

That must be how Mom did it, Scotti decided. She probably has subliminal messages in that Jazzer-cise tape she plays every day at the crack of dawn.

Scotti could not remember when she had felt so depressed. The more she thought about the whole situation, the worse it got. Was Lorna in on it, too? Was that whole mushing-the-mincerooms number staged so that the two of them could have time alone in the kitchen to plot? And what about Ann. Wasn't she doing everything in her power to keep Scotti from wanting to move back home? Fixing fabulous food? Even finding a New York publisher for her novel?

A novel, Scotti thought. That's what this whole thing sounds like. And once it's over, I'll write one about my experiences. I'll call it *Paths of Deception*, and I'll be the beautiful and tragic heroine.

At the sound of a car pulling into the driveway, Scotti sat up. It would be Ann coming home from work. Ann would be expecting her to be ecstatic over the newspaper advertisement about the New York publisher's representative and the chance to get her novel published.

Scotti got up and hurried into the bathroom to survey herself in the mirror. "Gross!" she said. The face that looked back at her had dull blue eyes and a miserable expression. She couldn't let Ann see her this way.

Splashing cold water on her face, Scotti tried to smile. It would be a fake smile, of course, pasted onto her face for Ann's benefit. But no matter how hard she pushed, the corners of her mouth refused to budge from their downturned position. She sighed and poked an index finger into each corner, forcing them up, but the instant she removed them, her sad expression returned. In final desperation she pulled her lips wide, exposing her newly straightened teeth.

At the sight of herself, Scotti burst out laughing. "I look like a snarling dog," she cried through her laughter. This time the smile remained. It's okay now, she thought. I can face Ann and the rest of the Markhams.

The kitchen was a madhouse when Scotti entered a few minutes later. The only one calm was Tiffany, who stood in front of the television set intently watching Bill Cosby consume a bowl of Jell-O instant chocolate pudding. Skip and his father were beside the microwave oven where Mrs. Markham popped a casserole inside and began talking excitedly, waving her hands for emphasis.

"It's the most exciting thing in the world," she cried. "Our own Scotti is going to show her novel to a New York publisher! Can you imagine that? OUR OWN SCOTTI! Oh! Here she comes now!"

Scotti managed an embarrassed little smile as she walked into the room. What Ann was saying was true. Scotti was going to show *Prisoner of Fate* to a publisher's representative and maybe get it published. It was what she had dreamed of, and suddenly she wondered why she had spent so much time worrying about Lorna going to Hawaii when her own greatest ambition was about to come true. Not only that, but Skip was looking at her, and he was smiling as if he thought she was someone important. Coy Markham was smiling, too, and he stepped forward as she got near and wrapped a huge arm around her.

"Well, little darlin', this is just about the best news I've heard in a long time. We're going to have a famous author living right here in this house with us. People will probably start lining up at the front door to get your autograph."

Scotti's heart was pounding. Would people really ask for her autograph? What if Skip asked? Should she just sign her name, or should she write a message the way everyone always did in autograph books? If she wrote a message, what would she write? "Roses are red; violets are blue; I'm writing a romance novel;

about me and you"? Gross! On second thought, she decided, she would sign it "Little Darlin'." She would give nearly anything if he would call her by the same name his parents used. Maybe if she signed her autograph that way he would take the hint, she thought, glancing toward Skip. To her delight, he was still looking at her appraisingly.

He leaned back on the counter, resting on an elbow, and said with a chuckle, "Once you get rich and famous, you probably won't have anything to do with people like us."

"Oh, no!" Scotti protested. "That's not true. I'll always like you. Nothing could ever change that. Honest. I'll even give you an autographed copy of my book absolutely free."

No one said anything, and Scotti felt a blush spread over her face as she looked into Skip's eyes and saw that he was teasing. He knows how I feel about him, she thought miserably, and he just made me admit it.

"Scotti really does like you, Skippy," piped up Tiffany, who had turned off the television set and joined them. "I know she does because I saw her looking—"

"TIFFANY!" Scotti cried. "Why don't you tell them the big news you told me about Lorna."

Tiffany put her hands on her hips and glared at Scotti. "I am going to tell them about Lorna as soon as I finish telling them about—"

"Hey, Tiff. What's your big news?" asked Skip. He had a funny look on his face, as if he didn't want to hear about what Scotti had been looking at either, and she sighed deeply and said a silent prayer of thanks.

Tiffany had the spotlight now, and she gazed around importantly and began to talk. "Well, you see, Pete is terribly sick and so SOMEONE has to take the airplane to Hawaii this weekend, and Captain and Mrs. Wheeler are going to do it, and Lorna gets to go along to see what it's really like to be part of an airline family."

Tiffany looked from face to face as if she were expecting applause, but each of the Markhams turned a puzzled gaze on Scotti.

"It's probably true," she said. "Mom and Dad have enough seniority to take the Hawaii run when some of the regulars get sick. And they get free passes, so Lorna is probably going to use one of them."

"Oh my," Ann exclaimed, visibly impressed. "Wouldn't that be a treat for Lorna, but I wonder why Helene hasn't called me about it."

At that exact moment the phone rang, and Scotti could tell by Ann's part of the conversation that Hawaii was exactly what they were talking about. Scotti turned away, not wanting to hear any more of what they were saying. Her novel had been instantly forgotten as the Markhams' speculated about Lorna's trip to Hawaii all through dinner.

"I'll bet she'll get to go surfing," said Skip, and Scotti could hear a hint of jealousy in his voice.

"She'll probably need some new clothes—at

least a new bathing suit," Ann said softly to herself.
"And that's an awfully long flight. I wonder if she'll get
airsick. I'd better call the doctor for a prescription first
thing in the morning."

"A-yan, we'll need to put her spending money
into traveler's checks, darlin'," said Mr. Markham.
"You know how those resorts are full of pickpockets
and purse snatchers."

"I'll bet she'll see Magnum," cried Tiffany, her
face aglow. "Don't you think she'll see Magnum,
Scotti? You've been to Hawaii."

"Sure, Tiff. She'll probably see Magnum lots of
times."

Scotti finished eating and excused herself, scuffing off to Lorna's room. She knew that she should
stay to help with the dishes, but the same feeling of
depression that she had had when she first heard that
Lorna was going to Hawaii was sweeping over her
again. It didn't seem fair. It was bad enough that
Lorna was getting a trip that should have been hers,
but it was happening at the same time that Scotti
would be showing her novel to the New York publisher. Everybody had forgotten about that already.
All anybody could think about was Lorna. Nobody
even cared about her anymore.

Scotti awakened sometime later, surprised that
she had fallen asleep across Lorna's bed. The room
was dark, and only a thin stream of moonlight fell
between the half-open drapes at the window. She
yawned and looked at the clock beside the bed. The
red digital readout blinked 9:03 . . . 9:03 . . . 9:03.

Scotti frowned and turned the clock to the wall. It had been hours since she had got up from dinner. Everyone else was probably in the family room watching television, but no one had knocked on her door to see if she wanted to join them. Why should they? They had Lorna and her trip to Hawaii to talk about. They didn't need her.

She parted the drapes and looked out across the back lawn. Things looked unreal in the moonlight. Shadows from the trees cut lightning bolts of black across the grass, which took on a soft, pearly glow. Above the tall stockade fence that separated the Markhams' property from her family's, the roof of her own familiar house peaked upward. I wonder what they're doing over there, she thought.

Taking a deep breath, Scotti raised the window and climbed onto the dew-covered lawn. It was a short sprint to the gate in the stockade fence. Before she opened it, Scotti glanced back toward the Markhams' house. All the drapes were drawn. Good, she thought. They'll never know I'm gone.

The gate had a perpetual squeak, and she opened it very slowly, hoping that the sound would be too faint for anyone to hear. Once through, she almost turned around and went back to the Markhams'. Her worst fears were coming true. Through the curtainless window in the kitchen she could see her parents and Lorna sitting around the table poring over brochures and maps.

Hawaii, she thought sourly. Not only that, but all three were smiling and talking excitedly, and every so often Lorna would let out a burst of laughter. The gaiety only stopped when Scotti saw her mother answer the phone and then hand the receiver to Lorna.

Standing there in the moonlight, Scotti felt that she had been totally forgotten. While Lorna talked on the phone, her parents continued to look at the travel brochures and smile at each other. It's as if I don't even exist, she thought, and a burst of tears flooded her eyes.

She stood there for a long time until finally a tiny feeling of determination began to grow and push aside her hurt and anger. She slapped away her tears with the back of her hand. "Who needs parents, anyway? I'll become a famous author," she whispered, "and spend all my time signing autographs and appearing on the Today Show and Good Morning, America. I'll show them."

16

Lorna's heart had pounded wildly as she watched Mrs. Wheeler hang up the phone and turn toward her earlier in the evening. She had held her breath all through the conversation between the two mothers.

"She says it's perfectly all right for you to go to Hawaii with us!" Mrs. Wheeler danced over to where Lorna stood beside the kitchen table and gave her a big hug. "I knew she would. I just knew it."

In a daze Lorna sank into a chair. She knew that Mrs. Wheeler was still talking, and was even aware that she was saying something about Scotti, but she was too overcome with surprise to listen. Although it had only been a few hours since Mrs. Wheeler's lunchtime announcement about the Hawaii trip, it seemed to Lorna as if days, even weeks, had passed. They had had to wait until evening when Ann Markham returned home from her job for Office

Temps and then, each time Mrs. Wheeler had reached for the phone, Lorna had asked her to wait a little longer. Lorna knew her mother's moods. She was always tired and grouchy when she first got home from work. And then she didn't like to be interrupted while she was preparing dinner, especially if she was trying to follow a long and complicated recipe.

By the time Lorna finally nodded to Mrs. Wheeler that the time was right to make the call, she had gathered a long list of reasons why her parents would probably say no. First was the fact that Lorna would be taking a trip without her parents. It was weird, but just as Mrs. Markham did not want Tiffany to be near a swimming pool unless she was there to supervise, the Markham children were not allowed to travel without at least one parent along. The Wheelers were parents, of course, but that had not made the slightest bit of difference when Skip had wanted to go on a fishing trip with Dave Norbert, Dave's father, and his father's poker club a couple of summers ago, so why would it matter now?

And then there was her mother's favorite four-letter word: FAIR. She could hear her now. "But Lorna, you know that if we let you go to Hawaii, it wouldn't be FAIR to Skippy or Tiffany, and you know how we always try to be FAIR to everybody in this family." Lorna had worried over this reason for a long time. Why was it that nobody ever seemed to notice when something wasn't FAIR to her? "Besides," her mother would probably add, "we've given you the special treat of spending two weeks with the Wheelers while Skippy and Tiffy haven't gotten any special treats at all. You'll have to admit that isn't FAIR."

But now the suspense was over, and her parents had actually agreed to let her go. Lorna came out of her trance just in time to see the Wheelers piling travel brochures onto the kitchen table where the remnants of dinner had been only moments before.

"Come on, Lorna," said Captain Wheeler. "This is your first trip to Hawaii, so we've got to make some plans."

For the next few hours they pored over pictures of Waikiki Beach and read descriptions of luaus with illustrations of grass-skirted hula girls and men wearing brightly colored aloha skirts.

"We'll get in on Friday afternoon and check into our hotel, and then we'll have the rest of Friday, Friday night, and all day Saturday to see the sights before we fly back Saturday night," said Mrs. Wheeler. She was busily making a list of all the places that were absolute "musts" to see.

"Don't forget to add lots of beach time," Lorna said dreamily. Ever since the first moment Mrs. Wheeler had mentioned going to Hawaii, she had been visualizing the beach with all the gorgeously tanned boys riding the waves on their surfboards and soaking up rays on the sand. The beach would be wall-to-wall hunks. She knew it from the pictures in the brochures.

If she could just meet one. The idea made her heart pound with excitement. Romance in Hawaii! Scotti might write novels about romance, but she,

Lorna Markham, was on her way to the real thing. She closed her eyes, imagining what her dream boyfriend would look like. He would be special, not another tourist or a boy from the mainland who looked as if he could be from her own school. No, he would be a handsome, dark-haired Hawaiian, tanned to a beautiful bronze, like the ones in the brochures. And after she returned home, they would write to each other and exchange photographs, and she would be the envy of every girl she knew—especially Scotti Wheeler. Maybe she would let Scotti interview her and write about her special romance in her next novel, Lorna thought with a chuckle.

Helene Wheeler frowned and chewed on the end of her pencil as she gazed at her list. "We could go to the beach Saturday afternoon, but that would mean giving up the Polynesian Culture Center, or we could see Pearl Harbor on Friday afternoon and go to the beach Saturday morning. That way we could still get up to the Polynesian Culture Center."

Captain Wheeler chuckled and winked at Lorna before speaking to his wife. "I have a feeling that Lorna may be a bit more interested in seeing the sights at the beach than the Culture Center or Pearl Harbor. Right, Lorna?"

Lorna felt her face redden. "Well, I—"

"Okay. I get the picture," said Mrs. Wheeler with a laugh. "Boys first, culture second. I understand."

The three of them were still laughing when the telephone rang. "It's after nine. I wonder who that could be," Helene Wheeler said as she reached for the phone. Her face brightened an instant later and she said, "It's for you, Lorna. It's your mom."

Lorna looked at the receiver in Mrs. Wheeler's outstretched hand as if it were a snake. Had her mother changed her mind about letting her go to Hawaii? What else could she want at this time of night?

"Hello," she said tentatively.

"Hi, darlin'. I just called to tell you how excited we all are about your trip to Hawaii. I hope you've remembered your manners and have thanked Captain and Mrs. Wheeler for inviting you along."

"Sure, Mom," Lorna lied, vowing to herself that she would thank them the instant she hung up the phone. "Is that all you wanted?"

"Of course not. Your daddy and I have been talking this whole trip over, and we're going to get traveler's checks so that your money will be safe from pickpockets and purse snatchers, and I'm going to call Doctor Peterson first thing in the morning and get a prescription for air-sickness pills just in case . . ."

Lorna sighed, only half-listening. Why did her mother always have to take all the fun out of things by being so practical?

". . . and I hope you understand about Scotti. Trips to Hawaii can come up anytime, especially in an airline family, but Friday is going to be a once-in-a-lifetime experience for her."

"What?" asked Lorna. "What about Scotti? What are you talking about?"

Tiny prickles started up her spine as she heard

her mother sigh and say in an exasperated tone, "Don't you know? I thought surely Helene would tell you."

"I'm not sure," Lorna hedged, remembering that Mrs. Wheeler had said something about Scotti, but she had been too much in shock to listen. "What was it again?"

"Well, darlin', it's just the most wonderful thing in the world. And when Helene suggested that Scotti go along to Hawaii with all of you and I told her about it, she agreed that it was a lot more important than any old trip."

"Mother! What is it?"

"Why, Scotti is going to show her novel to a New York publisher. Isn't that wonderful? Our own Scotti is going to become a famous author at thirteen. Now that's what I call maximizing her potential!"

Lorna reeled, feeling as if she had just been dashed with a gigantic bucket of cold water. Scotti was going to get her novel published? Her mother was right. What was a lousy weekend in Hawaii compared to that? Her dream of finding a handsome boyfriend in Hawaii was just that—a dream, but Scotti's dream of publishing her novel was about to come true.

"That's great," Lorna said weakly. "Tell her I said congratulations. Talk to you later, Mom. Bye."

Numbly, Lorna replaced the phone on the hook and glanced at the Wheelers. They were still poring over the brochures and were scarcely aware of her at all. She excused herself, saying that she suddenly felt exhausted from all the excitement, and escaped to Scotti's room. The house seemed strangely quiet. She was used to Tiffany cartwheeling through the halls and Skip playing his stereo at the maximum decibel level.

Her arms and legs felt as if they were weighted with stones as she threw herself across the pastel-and-white-striped bedspread. *My parents are probably glad to be shipping me off to Hawaii now that they have Scotti for a daughter,* she thought dismally. *They're only interested in daughters who maximize their potentials anyway. Look at the way Mom spoils Tiffany, and Tiff could read practically from the day she was born, and she's always talking about what she wants to be when she grows up.*

Lorna lay there for a long time thinking how her mother must really hate having her for a daughter. *I'm probably the biggest disappointment in her life,* Lorna decided. *Biggest!* she thought angrily. *I'm that, all right. Maybe she would like me a little more if I were small like Scotti.*

Rolling over onto her back, Lorna could feel hot tears rolling down her temples and into her hair. *Who needs parents, anyway? I'll go to Hawaii and find a gorgeous boyfriend, and maybe I won't even come back. I'll bet they'd be sorry then.*

17

Lorna awoke Tuesday morning with a new sense of determination. She divided her time for the next three days between preparing for her trip to Hawaii and stunting her growth with the assortment of junk foods stashed on the floor of Scotti's closet.

The instant coffee was the worst. Each morning it became harder to march into the bathroom with the jar of coffee, the mug, and the spoon and actually force herself to drink the awful stuff. By Wednesday. she had devised a plan that made it a little easier. Before actually putting the cup to her lips, she would wet her toothbrush and load it with an enormous glob of paste. Then, holding the brush at the ready in one hand, she would lift the mug to her mouth with the other. By thrusting the toothbrush into her mouth and brushing like crazy the instant the last drop of coffee was swallowed, she eliminated most of the bitter after-taste.

This had better work, she thought each time she set down the empty mug. Then she would stare at the wretched face in the mirror, her mouth foaming with green bubbles, and say a little prayer.

Back in Scotti's room she would down three handfuls of Count Chocula presweetened cereal before heading for Helene Wheeler's nutritious breakfast. She would gorge herself with potato chips and dill pickles before going to lunch, and chocolate bars and marshmallows killed her appetite for supper. If Mrs. Wheeler noticed that Lorna wasn't eating much at mealtime, she didn't say anything, and Lorna would hurry back into her room at bedtime and measure herself against the mark she had put on the wall.

Lorna tried to fill the rest of her time planning her wardrobe for the trip, making certain that she had at least three outfits for every possible occasion. No matter how hard she tried, though, she couldn't keep the memory of her mother's excitement over Scotti and her novel from invading her thoughts. *I wonder what she's doing over there?* Lorna couldn't help thinking. *She's probably planning all the ways she'll spend the money her book will earn. Or worse yet, she's probably decided that since she's going to be rich and famous, she doesn't want to waste time on someone like me. Well, I wouldn't call her for anything. She'd probably act like some kind of big deal. Let her call me.*

But Scotti didn't call. Lorna's mother did instead. "Lorna, this is your mother," Ann Markham said when Lorna answered the phone on Tuesday morning. "I just have a few things I want to remind you of. Your daddy and I are sending along plenty of money for you to pay your own way. Now be sure to pay for all your own meals. There is no reason for Mr. and Mrs. Wheeler to have to feed you. And darlin', please don't order more than you can eat. You know how bad you are about ordering everything on the menu and then picking at your food."

Lorna rolled her eyes toward the ceiling and said, "Yes, Mom, I'll remember. I'll pay for my own food and I'll only order what I can eat."

That afternoon, the phone rang again. It was for Lorna, but it wasn't Scotti calling. It was her mother again.

"Sweetheart, now don't forget to bring your little sister a present. I know how busy you'll be and everything, but little Tiffy would be crushed if you forgot to bring her something. Just any little thing will make her happy. Promise you won't forget?"

Lorna had to unclench her teeth to answer. "I promise, Mom. You know I wouldn't forget a thing like that."

On Wednesday Mrs. Markham called to instruct her on how to cash the traveler's checks she had dropped off earlier in the day. On Thursday there were three calls. One about how to tip in restaurants. One about watching out for pickpockets and purse snatchers EVEN THOUGH her money was in traveler's checks. But the last one was the absolute worst.

"Lorna, darlin', this is your mamma. I know how busy you are tonight getting ready to leave in the morning, but your daddy and I hope you have a good trip, and Lorna—" she paused, and Lorna felt her throat tighten as she waited for what would come next. "Don't forget to stand up straight and be proud of the tall Texan that you are. After all, you're going to be representing all of us over there."

Lorna nearly dropped the phone. I'm not going to a foreign country, for Pete's sake, she thought, but she didn't say it out loud. Can't she ever stop hassling me? Lorna wondered. Well, she's got Scotti now, she thought angrily. That ought to make her happy.

After she had hung up the phone, she made a final check of the mark on the wall and breathed a huge sigh of relief. At least one thing was going her way. She hadn't grown even a fraction of an inch.

Scotti, too, faced with determination her first full week with the Markhams and the prospect of showing her novel to a New York publisher. So what if her parents were taking someone else to Hawaii? She would spend all of her time and energy becoming a world-famous novelist.

Ann had called the telephone number in the advertisement and had set up an appointment for ten o'clock Friday morning. "I've already told Office Temps that I won't be able to work for them that day, and I've made arrangements for Tiffany to play at a friend's house," she assured Scotti. "That way I can be right there with you, darlin', so that you won't be too nervous."

Well, at least someone cares enough to be with me, Scotti thought as she faced the job of getting her novel into shape to show to the publisher.

Eeks! I really ought to type it, she thought with a stab of panic. But I don't have a typewriter, and even if I did it would take forever to type a hundred and ninety-one pages with two fingers. Still, with Friday only three days away, the task of recopying it all by hand was too great. She opted for rewriting only those pages where something was marked out, the writing was especially sloppy, or food stains made the words illegible.

That still left seventy-nine pages to rewrite, and as Scotti propped herself up on Lorna's bed on Tuesday afternoon to start the tedious job, she couldn't help wondering what Lorna was doing. Scotti made a face. She's probably out shopping for a new wardrobe so that she can show off even more when she gets back from her trip.

Gritting her teeth with renewed purpose, Scotti scanned page 7, the first page she had pulled out to recopy.

The beautiful Dianna sank into the grass beside the bubbling stream totally unaware of the beauty all around her. Her heart was heavy, and tears began streaming down her face. Soon her head was resting on a mound of ferns growing beside the stream as sobs racked her body. Her thoughts were on Maude and the terrible scene that had just taken place between them.

"Oh, why doesn't she understand or care about me?" Dianna cried, but the warble of a bird was her only answer.

18

Lorna fidgeted in her seat at Gate 32 at the Dallas-Fort Worth Airport on Friday morning. The sign above the podium proclaimed that this was Flight 5 departing for Honolulu at 9:55 A.M. Although there was still more than an hour until flight time, several other passengers were already seated in the lounge area. Helene Wheeler had explained that they were arriving at the airport so early because Captain Wheeler had to go through a preflight check in the cockpit, and that she needed to board early also to make certain that the meals had been loaded and the plane was in readiness for its passengers.

In spite of the hurt and frustration of the past few days, Lorna felt excitement growing now that she was about to board the plane for her first trip to Hawaii. As she hurried along the snakelike jetway that connected the terminal to the plane once the announcement to board was made, she tried not to think about the fact that she would be sitting alone. Both Captain and Mrs. Wheeler would be busy, of course, and Mrs. Wheeler had reminded her at least six times to be sure to push the attendant-call button if she needed anything at all. Still, Lorna could not get rid of the queasy feeling in the pit of her stomach at the thought of being on her own for the entire eight-hour flight, especially since it was only the third time she had been in an airplane in her entire life.

Surprisingly, the time passed quickly. From her window seat, Lorna watched the earth drop away at take-off. Before she had finished looking at the magazine tucked into the seat pocket in front of her, Mrs. Wheeler and the other attendants, dressed in Hawaiian costumes made in bright island prints, were in the aisles with the beverage carts. After that a lunch was served, consisting of salad, some sort of chicken in a sauce, plus nutritious-looking vegetables. Lorna pushed her plate aside, ate only the roll and butter and the chocolate cake, and then settled back to watch the movie on the screen in the center of the cabin. Right after the movie was over, Captain Wheeler's voice came over the loudspeaker announcing that the temperature in Honolulu was eighty-five and that they would be landing in approximately twenty minutes. Lorna felt a silly grin spread across her face and she looked quickly into her lap so that no one would see.

It was all she could do to keep from hugging herself with joy. Not only was she really going to Hawaii, she was almost there.

* * *

Scotti staggered into the bathroom on Friday morning and splashed water onto her face. Her eyes were a little puffy and red around the rims, but it was no wonder, she thought. She had worked until 3:17 in the morning to finish copying the sloppy pages of her manuscript, and not only did she look as if she had been up all night, her head felt that way, too.

In the shower, she let the refreshing water flood over her as she thought about *Prisoner of Fate*. It was a great book. She knew it was. Poor Dianna, she thought. So beautiful and so tragic, mistreated and misunderstood by her wicked mother, Maude the Tyrant, until suddenly, at the very end, she is carried off by her true love to live happily ever after in beautiful Markham Castle. Scotti giggled nervously. Maybe she should have called it something besides Markham Castle. When the book was published Skip would surely read it, and then he would know that she had written a love story about the two of them.

Scotti shook her head. It's too late now, she thought. She could never recopy all the pages where she had written "Markham Castle" before her appointment at ten o'clock, even if she wanted to. Besides, she thought dreamily, maybe reading my book will help Skip see me for what I really am.

Dressing quickly in her most authorish outfit—a navy-blue pleated skirt and a white blouse with a red, white, and blue polka-dot tie—she hurried down to breakfast, even though she knew that she was far too nervous to eat.

"Morning, darlin'," Ann called as she waved a pancake turner in Scotti's direction. "All set for the big day?"

Scotti nodded and stared at the stack of blueberry pancakes Ann was piling onto her plate. She could never eat all that. She would barf. All over the representative of the New York publisher. In fact, the very sight of them made her want to barf.

"You'd better eat your breakfast so that your tummy won't growl and make you 'barrassed. Right, Mom?" Tiffany sang out.

"That's right," Ann said. "You wouldn't want your stomach to growl right in the middle of your meeting with that New York publisher."

The thought of embarrassing herself was becoming a stronger and stronger possibility no matter whether she ate her breakfast or not, but Scotti breathed one small sigh of relief. At least she didn't have to face Skip right now. His breakfast plate, empty except for a pool of syrup, sat across from her, which meant that he had already left the table and was probably heading for work.

Just then the backdoor opened and Skip came sauntering in. "Forgot my lunch," he said, tipping his cowboy hat to his mom. Reaching for his lunch on the kitchen counter, he stopped and looked straight at Scotti, causing her to catch her breath.

Skip stood there for what seemed like hours to Scotti before he gave her a quick grin and said, "How's it going, kid?" Then he turned and disappeared out the door.

Scotti's scalp began to tingle as if a thousand daddy longlegs spiders were dancing in her hair. It was an omen, she thought. It had to be. After all, Skip was the hero of her book, and he had talked to her just before her appointment with the New York publisher's representative. It was a good-luck omen for sure.

The glow stayed with her all through breakfast, all through the ride to the Amfac Hotel at the Dallas-Fort Worth Airport, and right up to the moment, at 9:55 A.M., that she entered the waiting room on the fourteenth floor.

19

"Aloha and welcome to Hawaii." The taxi driver who spoke the words was short and round, and only the smile on his face was brighter than the colors in his shirt.

"Aloha," responded the Wheelers.

Aloha, thought Lorna. It was such a happy-sounding word, and it was in the air everywhere. She had heard it from the moment she stepped off the plane. People were calling it out to one another from every direction. "Aloha. Aloha."

She fingered the fragrant flower lei made of white tuberoses and red carnations that Captain Wheeler had bought for her at the airport and watched the tiny taxi driver load their luggage into his cab. She felt certain that she truly was in paradise. She could hardly wait to get to the hotel, change into her swimming suit, and head for Waikiki Beach.

Traffic was heavy as they drove past the turnoff

for Pearl Harbor and through downtown Honolulu toward their hotel. Lorna took everything in—the suntanned people in bright print clothes, the palm trees, the occasional glimpses of the ocean. Everything. Finally, the taxi pulled up to the hotel. The smiling taxi driver held the door for her to get out.

"Aloha," he said again. "Have a very pleasant stay."

"Aloha," said Lorna, giggling self-consciously as she looked down at him. It was almost like speaking a foreign language. This is going to be fun, she thought.

Captain Wheeler checked them in. "We're on the nineteenth floor overlooking the ocean," he said as they boarded the elevator. "Lorna, you'll have your own room with a connecting door to ours."

Lorna smiled and accepted the key he held out to her. Her very own hotel room in Hawaii. The elevator stopped on the third floor, and four people got on. Three were Oriental and the fourth looked to be a native Hawaiian with the same dark hair and skin as the man who had driven their taxi. Another thing struck Lorna. She was taller than all of them. Slumping forward and bending her knees slightly, she concentrated on watching the floor numbers roll by and finally stop on nineteen.

Lorna got her first glimpse of the surf when she stepped onto the beach at Waikiki a little while later. It was even more beautiful than she had imagined it would be. The water was a deep shade of blue, and the waves that began forming far offshore became gigantic swells before unfolding in sprays of white foam that carried surfers toward the beach. Lorna held her breath as she watched swimmers belly flop onto their boards, paddle out to deep water, and wait until the next wave was underneath their surfboards. Then they would spring up, balance precariously on the boards, and ride them in to shore.

"Lorna! We're over here."

Mrs. Wheeler was calling to her. The Wheelers had found a spot on the crowded beach near the water and had already spread three beach mats on the sand. Lorna raced to join them.

"I can't believe that I'm really here," she gushed as she stripped off the shirt and shorts she had worn over her bathing suit and dropped onto the empty mat beside them. "Me, Lorna Markham. I'm actually lying on the beach at Waikiki. It's fantastic!"

Mrs. Wheeler laughed. "You're here, all right. And you'd better let me spread some suntan lotion on your back. This tropical sun is stronger than you're used to, and if you aren't careful, you'll get a bad burn."

Obediently, Lorna handed over her suntan lotion and turned her back toward Mrs. Wheeler. It was the perfect opportunity to survey the beach for cute guys. She spotted four absolutely gorgeous hunks lounging together on beach towels near the water, but an instant later her excitement fizzled as she realized that two of them had mustaches and one a full red beard, meaning that they were far too old for her. That's okay, she thought. It's a big beach and it's crowded with people. Unfortunately, the boy she was looking for—the gorgeous, suntanned Hawaiian— was nowhere to be seen.

Lorna turned her left side to Mrs. Wheeler and surveyed a new section of beach. There, too, were older men with protruding stomachs, fathers taking toddlers to the water's edge, and an assortment of otherwise unsuitable males, but nowhere could she find the one she was searching for.

Disappointed, she turned her gaze back to the water. The surfers were still bobbing and weaving and riding their boards atop gigantic waves that came crashing toward shore. Then she saw him. With dark glistening hair and a deep tan he was definitely Hawaiian, and he wore bright-blue trunks. The best surfer of all, he stood on his board with arms outstretched and laughed into the wind. He was so handsome that Lorna caught her breath as he rode out the wave, stopped in shallow water, and then paddled to deep water again. She watched him ride wave after wave, always laughing and never toppling into the surf. If only he would come onto the beach.

"Come on. Let's get wet." Helene Wheeler jumped to her feet and waited for Lorna. Lorna scrambled up and followed her. Maybe this is it, she thought, my big chance.

The beach was crowded, and Lorna picked her way through the people. She was able to walk without losing sight of her handsome Hawaiian, but his attention was on surfing and he never once looked toward the beach.

After the hot sun, the water felt refreshing, and

she and Mrs. Wheeler took turns splashing each other and ducking into the foamy breakers. Finally, they headed back to their mats. Lorna cast one last glance toward the surfers. Rats! she thought. He's gone. How was he able to get away from me so quickly? She sank onto her beach towel feeling unbearably depressed.

"Lorna, honey," said Mrs. Wheeler. "Craig and I are going to take a walk along the beach. You don't mind if we leave you alone for a little while, do you?"

Lorna shook her head and watched them disappear into the crowd at the water's edge. Actually, she was glad they had left her alone. She certainly didn't feel like making conversation now. She had found him—the boy of her dreams—and now he was gone. Even worse, tomorrow they would be going home.

"Don't tell me. Let me guess. You just got to Hawaii today."

Startled, Lorna looked around to see if the friendly words were meant for her. Her heart stopped. Sinking onto the sand not three feet behind her was—HIM! The handsome Hawaiian surfer had come out of the water, and now he was talking to her.

Fighting not to blush she said, "How could you tell?"

He threw back his head and laughed. "It was easy. I even spotted you from the water. If you'd gotten here yesterday, you would be as red as a lobster. If you'd gotten here before that, you would be beginning to look like me. But since you're so white—" He laughed again and then said, "Aloha. My name is Kimo. Welcome to Hawaii."

"Hi, Kimo. I mean Aloha. My name is Lorna, and you're right. I did just get here today."

"Lorna?" he said, frowning and shaking his head, "I don't think there's a Hawaiian name that means Lorna. The closest one I know is Lala. That's Hawaiian for Laura, but I like Lorna better."

"Thanks," said Lorna. Her head was spinning, and this time she was certain she was blushing. She racked her brain for something to say. "Uh—is Kimo—I mean, does it mean something else?"

"It means Jim, but I prefer to be called Kimo."

"Oh, I don't blame you," she gushed. "I like it better too."

Kimo was even better looking up close than he had been from a distance, and his relaxed, friendly manner was beginning to put her at ease. He asked where she was from, and they talked about Texas for a while. He told her that he went to high school near Diamond Head.

"It's that big crater over there," he said, pointing to the tall, flat-topped mountain at the end of the island. The talk switched to favorites, and Lorna was surprised at how many things they had in common. Favorite rock stars—Duran Duran. Favorite movie actor—Matt Dillon. Favorite food—pizza.

"Do you mean to say that you eat pizza here in Hawaii?" Lorna asked in amazement.

"Of course," he teased. "This is America, you know."

They laughed and talked for a long time, and finally Kimo said the one thing Lorna had not even dared to hope he would say.

"If I give you my address, will you write me when you get home and send me your picture?"

"Sure, if you'll write back and send me a picture of you."

Her heart was pounding as she rummaged around in her beach bag until she found two scraps of paper and a ballpoint pen. It was so wonderful that she wished she could pinch herself to make sure she was really awake. When Kimo handed her his address, she folded it carefully and put it in the secret compartment of her wallet where it would be safe.

She felt a tap on her shoulder and looked around to see Helene Wheeler smiling down at her. Lorna hadn't noticed that the Wheelers had returned from their walk, but now they had both folded their mats and gathered towels and lotion. It can't be that late, she thought.

"I'm sorry, Lorna, but we really do have to be getting back to the hotel now." Mrs. Wheeler had a sympathetic look on her face, but that didn't stop the feeling of panic from rising in Lorna. She couldn't leave now—now that she had found Kimo.

He was smiling again. "Sorry you have to go," he said. "I'll look for you again tomorrow. And in case we miss each other then, we've got each other's address, right?"

"Right," Lorna said halfheartedly. She stood up,

gathered her things, and then suddenly remembered that she hadn't introduced Kimo to the Wheelers. "Oh, Kimo. This is Captain and Mrs. Wheeler. They're with the airline and they invited me along this weekend."

Kimo stood up, smiled broadly, and extended his right hand toward Captain Wheeler. "Aloha," he said. "I'm happy to meet you."

Lorna felt her mouth drop open as the two shook hands. Kimo—handsome, bronzed Hawaiian boy of her dreams—was at least an inch shorter than Captain Wheeler, and that made him two inches shorter than she was. It can't be true! Lorna thought wildly. It just can't!

They said good-bye, and Lorna and the Wheelers crossed the beach toward the entrance to the hotel. Lorna barely heard Helene Wheeler talking about what a nice young man Kimo seemed to be and how much fun it must be to meet a good-looking boy on the beach.

Lorna nodded. "But did you notice how short he is?" she was finally able to say.

"Sure," said Mrs. Wheeler as they stepped into the elevator. "Does it really matter?"

Lorna started to answer but caught herself. She had almost said, "You bet it does! I'm practically a head taller than he is." But she hadn't said it. And as she leaned against the back wall of the elevator and watched the floors race past, she was suddenly glad. What if Mrs. Wheeler had misunderstood and thought she was saying that there was something wrong with being short? That's just the opposite of how I really feel, Lorna thought. Scotti is short and she's my best friend. Captain and Mrs. Wheeler are both short, and look at what super people they are. I couldn't dislike somebody just because he was short.

The elevator stopped at the nineteenth floor, and Lorna realized that Helene Wheeler was still looking at her as if waiting for an answer to her question.

"Of course it doesn't matter that Kimo is shorter than I am," said Lorna, feeling a surge of new understanding. "Short and tall are only sizes. They have nothing to do with what a person is like inside."

Helene Wheeler flashed Lorna an approving smile and the three of them left the elevator and headed down the hallway toward their adjoining rooms. Lorna unlocked her own door and slipped inside.

Suddenly, she missed her parents terribly. She missed Skip and Tiffany, too. Tears flooded her eyes. They're tall Texans and proud of it, she thought, just the way I am. If only they were here, then I'd feel at home.

20

The large hotel room that Scotti and Ann entered was part of a suite of rooms and did not contain a bed. The furniture had been arranged so that straight-backed chairs ringed the walls to resemble a doctor's waiting room. Several other people, most of them looking as nervous as Scotti, were already seated, and all of them were clutching their manuscripts.

"May I help you?"

Scotti turned abruptly to the receptionist sitting at a desk to the right of the door they had entered. She was a tall, lean blond woman with blood-red lipstick and fingernails to match. From the woman's bored expression Scotti guessed that she didn't really care if she helped anyone or not.

"Go ahead, darlin'. Answer the lady," Ann whispered just above Scotti's left ear. "Don't be scared."

Scotti cleared her throat and shifted her manuscript from her left hand to her right, extending it slightly toward the young woman. "I have an appointment at ten o'clock to show my novel to—" She suddenly realized that she did not have the faintest idea of the name of the New York representative.

"To Ms. Shackelford," said the bored receptionist. Then she pointed a long red fingernail toward a clipboard. "Sign your name and have a seat. You'll be called when she's ready to see you."

Scotti picked up the yellow pencil and signed her name, noting that she was number eight on the list. Scotti wondered if they all had ten o'clock appointments or if Ms. Shackelford was simply running late.

Dropping into the nearest empty seat, Scotti surveyed the other waiting authors. Directly across the room was a large woman with a manuscript perched precariously on her knees. Scotti winced as the woman tugged at the hem of her skirt, trying to force it to cover more of her legs, and almost spilled the pages into the floor. Three chairs from the woman sat a man in a tight-fitting navy-blue suit. He was reading through his own book, moving his lips in an animated fashion as he read, and he appeared to be enjoying the story immensely. Scotti suppressed a giggle and glanced at Ann, but before Ann could respond, the buzzer on the receptionist's telephone sounded.

Glancing at the clipboard, the receptionist called out in a flat voice, "Mister Theodore Blo—Blogget."

The lip mover looked up, his eyebrows nearly shooting off the top of his head. "It's pronounced Blo-

JAY," he said as he quickly gathered his papers and scurried to her desk. "It's French, you know."

The receptionist looked unimpressed. "Go on in," she said, nodding toward the closed door behind her. Ms. Shackelford will see you now."

Scotti felt a tingling sensation and then a rumbling in the pit of her stomach. She hoped it wasn't the blueberry pancakes on the move. Mr. Blo-JAY had disappeared through the only door in the room besides the one she and Ann had come in through, which could only mean that in the case of an emergency there would be no bathroom to duck into. Still, her nervousness was increasing. Only seven more to go until her turn.

Ann must have noticed her uneasiness because she reached over and gave Scotti's hand a firm squeeze. Although Mr. Blo-JAY did not come out again, the buzzer sounded a few minutes later and this time the receptionist called a Miss Porter. A wisp of a lady carrying an enormous manuscript came forward and disappeared through the door behind the receptionist. One by one, the others were called into Ms. Shackelford's presence, leaving only Scotti and Ann in the waiting room. Scotti's heart was beginning to pound, and she fervently hoped that there was another exit in the adjoining room so that Ms. Shackelford was not devouring authors behind the closed door.

Scotti glanced at her watch. It was almost eleven o'clock, and a new stream of hopeful writers was filling the room. Just as a woman entered carrying a crying baby and a manuscript in one hand and dragging an unhappy toddler with the other, the buzzer sounded for the eighth time.

"Scotti Wheeler," the receptionist called over the baby's cries. Ms. Shackelford will see you now."

To Scotti's immense relief, Ann rose from her chair and gently nudged Scotti forward. "Let's go," she urged. "Your big moment is here."

Scotti's knees were shaking as she turned the knob and pushed open the door. This was it. She was meeting the representative of a New York publisher face to face.

Whatever Scotti had been expecting a publisher's representative to be, Ms. Shackelford definitely was not it. She was taller and leaner than the receptionist, with mounds of silver hair piled on top of her head and a roadmap of deep wrinkles covering her long, thin face. A silver-and-turquoise necklace the size of armor hung around her neck, and matching earrings cascaded to her shoulders.

"Come in! Come in!" she called in a hoarse voice, and she rushed toward Ann, grabbing her hand and pumping it vigorously. "Welcome to Integrity Press. Today is the day you become a published author!"

"Oh, no!" sputtered Ann. "You've made a mistake. I'm not the author. Scotti is."

Surprise registered in Ms. Shackelford's eyes for an instant, but she recovered quickly. Turning to Scotti, her face seemed to take on a new glow. "How wonderful," she cooed. Then she put a firm hand on Scotti's shoulder, propelling her in the direction of a desk in the center of the room and pushing her down toward a waiting chair. Lowering her voice to confidential tones, she said, "You know, young lady, it is so sad that most parents neglect to see the budding genius in their children. You are truly blessed to have a mother who not only sees the promise of your future but is eager to help you achieve it."

Scotti clutched the manuscript in her lap as she struggled to comprehend the woman's words.

"Wrong again," said Ann, and Scotti detected the sound of irritation in her voice. "She isn't my daughter. She's—"

"A sister? A niece? No matter," said Ms. Shackelford, twirling triumphantly around the room until she stood behind her desk. "What's important is that you're here," she said. Then addressing Scotti directly, she added, "I presume that that is your wonderful manuscript in your lap."

Nodding, Scotti gingerly laid the manuscript on the edge of the desk. Ms. Shackelford picked it up and scanned the hand-printed cover. "*Prisoner of Fate,* by Scotti Wheeler. Scotti Wheeler! What a wonderful name for an author. It's a beautiful name. One an eager reader—a FAN—will easily remember."

She paused, and a picture flashed into Scotti's mind of a fan rushing into a bookstore, and she heard that fan asking the sales clerk for a book—any book— by her favorite author, Scotti Wheeler.

"Of course," Ms. Shackelford added slowly, "last

names that start with W are always relegated to the bottom shelf at the back of the store. What you need is a last name that starts with an F or a G or an H. First shelf, eye-level high. You must think of marketing, you know."

She paused again, and Scotti exchanged worried looks with Ann. What was Ms. Shackelford getting at?

"And Scotti. That name is all right, I suppose. But what you really need is something with more of a romantic sound, like Samantha. Samantha is a terribly popular name for novelists these days. Or Sabrina. SABRINA HAWTHORNE! That's it! *Prisoner of Fate,* by Sabrina Hawthorne. Now doesn't that sound better?"

Scotti squirmed nervously in her chair. This interview wasn't going at all the way she had expected. And she certainly didn't want "by Sabrina Hawthorne" on her book. No one would know that she had written it.

Ms. Shackelford had picked up a calendar and was thumbing through the pages and squinting. "I think we can schedule publication for the week of September fifteenth. Yes, I'm sure we can. Now how does that sound, my dear?"

Scotti was even more puzzled than ever. "But how do you know you want to publish my book? You haven't even read it."

Ms. Shackelford looked thoughtful for a moment. "Only the author knows the real value of a book," she said softly. Then she gazed into the distance with misty eyes, as if she were watching the American flag flutter in the breeze. "Our business at Integrity Press is to help you get it published."

Before Scotti could answer, Ms. Shackelford's mood changed abruptly, and she whipped out a long sheet of paper and thrust it toward Ann. "This is our contract," she said crisply. "As soon as Miss Wheeler's parents sign it and return it with a check for five thousand dollars, we will put her novel into immediate production. It's been nice meeting you. Good day."

Grabbing the contract from the woman's hand, Ann tore it into a million pieces and tossed it into the air like confetti. "There is your contract, and you know what you can do with it!" she stormed.

Scotti's heart dropped into her shoes as she gathered up her novel and shuffled toward the door. Integrity Press wasn't a real publisher at all, she thought. Not the kind she had dreamed would publish her novel, anyway. She had read about real publishers. They read your book first and then paid you money to publish it if they liked it.

"I'm really sorry, honey," said Ann. She draped an arm around Scotti's shoulder as they waited for the elevator.

Ann squeezed Scotti's hand, and Scotti squeezed back. All she wanted to do was cry, but she bit her lip and sniffed back her tears before Ann could see. Ann had been wonderful. She had thought the ad was for a real publisher, and she had taken off from work so that Scotti could show the representative her book. She had even saved Scotti from the clutches of Ms. Shackelford and Integrity Press. Still, Scotti held back her tears. What she longed for now was the familiar feeling of her own mother's arms around her. Then she would be able to cry.

21
___

Scotti spent Friday afternoon and all day Saturday working on *Journey to the Stars*. The disappointment over Ms. Shackelford and Integrity Press was beginning to wear off. After all, she reasoned, thirteen *was* a little young to become a famous author. And the more she thought about it, the more she was certain that *Journey to the Stars* was really going to be a much better novel than *Prisoner of Fate*. She would wait until it was finished and then show it to a real New York publisher. Maybe she would use one of her parents' airline passes to go to New York. Maybe, she thought wistfully, she would even ask her parents to go along.

She was so absorbed in her writing that she did not hear the telephone ring Sunday morning.

"Scotti. Telephone. It's your mamma," Ann called through the closed bedroom door.

Scotti raced for the phone. "Hi, Mom. When did

you get home?" she asked excitedly. Then she paused and added more slowly, "How was Hawaii?"

"We just walked in the door from the airport. And Hawaii was lovely. As usual. But it would have been nicer if you could have been there. Of course, I understand. When Ann told me about your appointment with the New York publisher's representative, I knew you'd want to stay in Texas. Tell me all about the appointment. How did it go?"

Scotti let her mother's words sink in for a moment. Was it possible that her parents HAD wanted her to go to Hawaii after all and that she had simply misunderstood?

"Oh . . . uh . . . the appointment," she sputtered. She started to make the big speech she had been practicing and say that she had had the chance to publish her novel with Integrity Press but had turned it down. After all, it was true. But instead she sighed deeply and said, "Not so well. They would only publish it if I would pay them five thousand dollars."

"Oh, Scotti. I'm so sorry."

She sounded so genuinely sorry that Scotti felt better instantly. "Oh, that's okay, Mom. I've started a new novel that's going to be even better. It's about astronauts, and it's called *Journey to the Stars*."

"Astronauts, eh? That sounds fascinating. Maybe you'll let your dad and me read it some time."

A tingle raced up Scotti's spine. Her mother was finally interested in her writing. "Sure," she said.

"And Scotti," her mother said softly. "Since you're working on another novel, what would you think of moving back home? I mean, I know how much you're enjoying staying with the Markhams and everything, but you'd have a lot more privacy here in your own room."

"And a lot more peace and quiet," Scotti said quickly. She knew that her voice sounded excited, but she couldn't help it. That was exactly the way she felt. It was too good to be true. She was going home, and she chattered on happily, telling her mother all about Ms. Shackelford, the bored secretary, and even Mr. Blo-JAY.

At the other end of the house, Lorna rushed in the backdoor. "I'm home," she called. "Mom? Dad? Tiffy? Skip? Is anybody home?"

An instant later, people appeared from every direction. Tiffany was first, and she tackled her sister around the knees and cried, "You're home! You're home! What did you bring me?"

Skip and her father came in from the garage wearing broad grins. "Hey, Lorna. Meet any good-looking surfers?" her brother asked.

"As a matter of fact, I did. So there," she said. "He was Hawaiian. His name was Kimo, and he was awfully handsome and awfully—" Lorna sighed.

"Awfully what, dear?" asked her mother.

Lorna looked at each one of them and began to giggle. "Awfully short for a tall Texan like me."

Everyone started to laugh and ask questions all at once. It was a super homecoming, and after the excitement died down Ann Markham put an arm around her daughter's shoulder. "Let's sit on the back porch for a few minutes before you go back to the Wheelers," she said.

Lorna could feel her mother looking her over from head to toe as they sat down in the padded redwood chairs. Was something wrong? she wondered.

Finally, her mother spoke. "Lorna, I hope you won't mind my saying so, darlin', but you look a little thin. I know that Mrs. Wheeler is a wonderful cook and very weight- and nutrition-conscious, but you look as if you could use a good home-cooked meal."

Lorna was so surprised that she couldn't say anything for a moment. Before she found her voice, her mother went on again. "Of course, I know you're having a wonderful time staying in Scotti's room, and we're certainly enjoying having Scotti with us, but . . . it would be awfully nice to have you back home."

Lorna thought her heart would burst with excitement. She was going home where she belonged, and the two of them sat talking until mosquitoes chased them inside.

After Scotti hung up from talking to her mother, she went back into Lorna's room and sprawled across the water bed. Her momentary excitement at the prospect of going back home had been replaced by a sudden, disturbing question. What was she going to say to Lorna? What excuse could she possibly use to get back into her own house and her own room practically a week early without hurting her best friend's feelings?

"After all the complaining I've done about my mom," Scotti reasoned aloud, "Lorna will get the wrong idea and think that I think her mom is WORSE!"

She flopped over onto her back, sending waves rippling across the surface of the bed. "And what will Ann think? As if I didn't know. She'll think that I blame her for Ms. Shackelford and Integrity Press and not getting *Prisoner of Fate* published."

Scotti's anguish deepened. "The truth is, I can't go home yet. Not until the two weeks are up. I'll just have to find a way to make Mom understand how hurt Lorna and her family would be if I moved out on them right now."

Tears found their way into Scotti's eyes as she thought about home and her parents and all the things she would miss. She was so full of misery that she barely heard the knock on the bedroom door.

"Yes?" she called, trying to sound as cheerful as she could. She couldn't let anyone know what she was going through.

"Scotti? It's me. May I come in?"

It was Lorna, but her voice had a faraway sound.

"I guess so," said Scotti. She didn't really want to talk to Lorna at this particular moment, but there was nothing else she could do.

Lorna entered the bedroom, and Scotti thought for an instant that her friend really had shrunk. But she was only slumping. Slumping not to look shorter, Scotti sensed, but because she had something important on her mind.

Scotti braced herself, but Lorna looked unbearably nervous. She cleared her throat. "Scotti, I just wanted to tell you that I think your parents are great," she began. "They treated me like their own daughter and they took me on a super trip and did everything they could for me, but—"

BUT? Scotti's heart did a triple somersault. Lorna had said her parents were great—BUT!

"But what?" she asked eagerly.

Lorna shifted her weight from her right foot to her left and looked at Scotti pleadingly.

"But I'd really like to come home. I know the two weeks aren't up yet, but would it hurt your feelings if I asked if we could swap back now?"

Scotti leaped off the water bed with such force that it rose in a tidal-wave swell. Then she threw her arms around her bewildered friend and hugged her.

"'I think your parents are great, too. And your mom's terrific for trying to help me get my novel published, and even Tiffany's not really so bad." Scotti couldn't get the words out fast enough. "And I want to go home, too!"

Suddenly words choked in her throat, and the two girls stood, arms still around each other, just looking at each other and sharing an unspoken moment.

It was Lorna who finally broke the silence. "I don't know how you stand vegetable lasagna all the time," she said, laughing. "You'll have to come over for barbequed brisket at least once a week."

"And this crazy water bed!" Scotti shrieked. "Don't you get seasick? Why not sleep over at my house some of the time?"

"Great. So tell me about your novel. Is it going to be published?"

"No, but I'll tell you about that later. First, I want to hear all about your trip."

By the time both girls moved all their things back to their own houses later that afternoon, jet lag had hit Lorna full force. It had been impossible to sleep during the "red-eye," as the overnight flight was called, and what little energy she had left had been spent greeting her family, answering all their questions about the trip, talking nonstop for almost two hours with Scotti, and now moving back home. All she really wanted to do was crawl into her bed and sleep, but she could hear her mother calling her.

"Lorna. Dinner's ready, darlin'."

She grinned sleepily at her face in the mirror. It's okay, she thought. It's my first home-cooked meal. It felt so good to be back home in her own house with her own family that nothing could bother her now. Not Tiffy. Not Skip. Not anything or anybody.

Scuffing down the hall, she dropped into her chair at the kitchen table and watched dreamily as her mother carried a platter of baked ham in her direction. She had forgotten how tall and pretty her mother was, and she was just about to tell her so when Ann Markham spoke first.

"Lorna, there you go slumping again. I would have thought that being in Hawaii would have made you notice how attractive people never slump. I just don't know what gets into you when you slump like that."

Instantly, she wasn't sleepy anymore. She gritted her teeth, nodded obediently to her mother, smiled, and drew herself up to her full height. She stayed tall and straight all through dinner and did not slump again until she was out of sight of the family and dialing Scotti's number on the phone.

"Scotti? This is Lorna. I have a very important question to ask."

"Shoot," said her petite friend.

"How are things now that you've moved back home?"

There was a pause and then Scotti said, "The pits. Mom caught me eating a candy bar and hit the ceiling. How about at your house?"

"The same. I slumped at the dinner table."

"Nothing's changed in spite of the Great Mom Swap," said Scotti with a sigh.

"You're right. That's why you have to meet me at the bus stop in a couple of minutes. It isn't dark yet. Your parents will let you out, won't they?"

"Only for a little while. But why meet there?"

"You'll see."

Five minutes later Lorna watched Scotti run breathlessly toward her. Between gulps of air she said,

"What was the emergency? I almost couldn't get out. Finally, I convinced Mom that I was going to jog off that candy bar."

"And she believed that YOU would JOG?" Lorna laughed heartily and then put an arm around Scotti's shoulder. "It's time to get serious," she said. Holding up a hand for silence, she sang, "My dog's shinier than your dog!"

Scotti's eyes brightened. "My dad can beat up your dad!"

Then in unison and at the top of their lungs they sang, "MY MOM'S CRABBIER THAN YOUR MOM!" and walked back home arm and arm.

ABOUT THE AUTHOR

BETSY HAYNES, the daughter of a former newswoman, began scribbling poetry and short stories as soon as she learned to write. A serious writing career, however, had to wait until after her marriage and the arrival of her two children. But that early practice must have paid off, for within three months Mrs. Haynes had sold her first story. In addition to a number of magazine short stories and the Taffy Sinclair series, Mrs. Haynes is also the author of *Spies on the Devil's Belt* and the highly acclaimed *Cowslip*. She lives in Colleyville, Texas, with her children and husband, a businessman who is the author of a young adult novel.

IT ALL STARTED WITH
THE
SWEET
VALLEY
TWINS

For two years teenagers across the U.S. have been reading about Jessica and Elizabeth Wakefield and their High School friends in SWEET VALLEY HIGH books. Now in books created especially for you, author Francine Pascal introduces you to Jessica and Elizabeth when they were 12, facing the same problems with their folks and friends that you do.

☐ **TAFFY SINCLAIR AND THE**   **15494/$2.50**
ROMANCE MACHINE DISASTER
by Betsy Haynes
Taffy Sinclair is furious. Her rival, Jana Morgan, has a date with Randy Kirwan, the most popular boy at school. When their teacher conducts a computer match-up game, Jana and 9 other girls, including Taffy turn out to be just right for Randy. Jana vows to win him! But is she any match for Taffy?

☐ **THE AGAINST TAFFY**   **15413/$2.50**
SINCLAIR CLUB
by Betsy Haynes
It was bad enough when Taffy Sinclair was just a pretty face. But now she's gone and developed a figure! This calls for drastic measures from the Against Taffy Sinclair Club made up of Jana Morgan and her four fifth-grade friends.

☐ **TAFFY SINCLAIR**   **15417/$2.50**
STRIKES AGAIN
by Betsy Haynes
It is time gorgeous Taffy Sinclair had a little competition. That's what Jana and her friends decide to give her when they form a club called The Fabulous Five. But when the club's third meeting ends in disaster, Jana finds she has four new enemies!

☐ **TAFFY SINCLAIR,**   **15330/$2.50**
QUEEN OF THE SOAPS
by Betsy Haynes
What could be worse? The snooty but perfectly gorgeous Taffy has done it again—she's won a part in a soap opera to play a beautiful girl on her deathbed. Nothing like this ever happens to Jana Morgan or her friends, and they're not going to stand being upstaged one more time!

WITTY ADVENTURES BY
FLORENCE PARRY HEIDE